T0068146

The Girl in the Mirror

Book 5

P. COSTA

THE GIRL IN THE MIRROR BOOK 5

Copyright © 2023 P. Costa.

All rights reserved. No part of this book may be used or reproduced by any means, graphic, electronic, or mechanical, including photocopying, recording, taping or by any information storage retrieval system without the written permission of the author except in the case of brief quotations embodied in critical articles and reviews.

This is a work of fiction. All of the characters, names, incidents, organizations, and dialogue in this novel are either the products of the author's imagination or are used fictitiously.

iUniverse books may be ordered through booksellers or by contacting:

iUniverse
1663 Liberty Drive
Bloomington, IN 47403
www.iuniverse.com
844-349-9409

Because of the dynamic nature of the Internet, any web addresses or links contained in this book may have changed since publication and may no longer be valid. The views expressed in this work are solely those of the author and do not necessarily reflect the views of the publisher, and the publisher hereby disclaims any responsibility for them.

Any people depicted in stock imagery provided by Getty Images are models, and such images are being used for illustrative purposes only. Certain stock imagery © Getty Images.

ISBN: 978-1-6632-5725-3 (sc)
ISBN: 978-1-6632-5726-0 (e)

Library of Congress Control Number: 2022912814

Print information available on the last page.

iUniverse rev. date: 10/18/2023

Dedication

This book is number five in a series of six in
which I hope readers can learn from.

We need to listen to our inner voice which comes from God
more often. We tend to forget what's really important.

The Navy

As she sat in the front seat with the recruiter, April could not help but wipe tears from her eyes. She blew her nose and controlled her breathing, but she dared not so much as picture her parents, Gordon and Miranda, in her mind, or she would begin to cry again.

"You're lucky," the recruiter said. "Some that I pick up have no one." No words were exchanged. It was too painful. It was like closing a door.

They rode to the bus station in silence where April would get on a bus and ride to the airport. There she would catch a flight to the base camp in Florida.

As she got on the bus, many things ran through her mind. Did she make the right decision? Would her parents be all right? With each question she could see the outcome, but not for herself. Now her life was in God's hands, whether good or bad. Now she had to rely on her skills and God. She knew that most people would think she was crazy if she said something like this out loud. These feelings were hers and hers alone, unless someone asked her, then she would cautiously share.

At the airport there were so many people scrambling to find gates and catch their designated flights. April took her time. She had forty five minutes to get to her gate. As she walked along, she bought a warm pretzel, and it reminded her of when she was in the Olympics. She checked her bag and guitar. Then she found her gate area, and sat down. Across the isle there were three soldiers in fatigues, one female and two males. They did not appear friendly or in the mood to talk, so April left them alone.

Before too long the lights began to light up and the counter person announced the flight would begin boarding. April got up taking her time in line she showed her ticket and was in the general passenger area. She found her seat in no time and sat down. She was at the window seat and soon someone sat down beside her, a couple filing in both seats to the isle.

He looked like a businessman. Both were well dressed, and April wondered why they would be seated in the economy section instead of first class.

The man caught her looking at him and he reached over to shake her hand saying, "Rupert Manning."

She shook his hand, "April D," she said.

His glasses were down further on his nose than they should be, and he asked her, "D Farms?"

"Yes," she said to him. "That's right."

"I know of them," he said. "I am a businessman and wanted to invest with them but was turned down."

April told him they did not want any business from outside, it needed to be centralized, like a family, like a whole.

The man nodded his head that he understood.

"Where are you headed?" April asked him.

"I am a consultant for a company that is campaigning for the next President of the United States," he told her.

"Wow, that's different," she said to him.

"I am very good with numbers, cause-and-effects, and can determine what a person should or should not do to win an election. Maybe someday you will run for a government position, if you do, call me. Even D Farms could use some assistance. You cannot win by just being liked, having experience, or being known. There are many factors that influence people," he said.

April was impressed. She never really thought about it before. In her hometown, running for a position was all based on knowing that person, their integrity, honesty, and willingness to help. She took his card and tucked it into her pocket.

The flight continued and the two of them exchanged conversation from time to time. It was Rupert Manning's turn to ask her, "So where are you headed?"

"I am heading to basic training at a Florida base. I am joining the Navy in hopes of becoming a Frogman or a Seal", she told him.

He looked at her as if she were not there. "Are you kidding?" he asked her.

"No sir. I assure you I am not. I feel this is my calling in life and if I don't do it, I will never know."

"Do you know what happens out there? I speak from experience. I was a Frogman in the 70s," he said to her.

"No, sir. I do not know everything, but I know that I am in my prime. I am a good athlete, and I am ready," she said to him.

Rupert Manning sat there stunned. He would never let his daughter do such a thing. As he sat there, he reminisced about what he read about this woman beside him. From what he remembered she was in the Olympics several times, and that was grueling training. He remembered when he joined. To be truthful nothing on earth would have prevented him from doing so, he had no right to discourage her and he apologized to her.

"It's all right. I know that because I am a woman many will feel I am not to be applying or try to be a Seal, and . . ."

Rupert interrupted her, "Now listen to me. There were times on our missions when we could have used a woman that was trained. Women have advantages with men that another man does not have. So you follow your dream. I hope it works out for you. It did for me, and I am not sorry.

The passengers slept for most of the flight, but April stayed awake. She could not have slept if she tried.

The plane touched down around 10:30 p.m. April stood up, taking her time, and waiting to get off the airplane. She stepped down the gangplank to the airport. It was a hub of soldiers and people alike, all scrambling to come in or leave. April collected her bag and guitar, bought a ticket to her base, and headed to a bus that would arrive at the base about 2:00 a.m.

The bus rattled on to the base and they all filed off as quickly as possible, lining up for inspection. The Drill Sergeant, Robert McCoy, was a short, black man who kept a small cigar in his mouth. He walked the line asking each recruit his name and where he was from. When finished, he told them that they would no longer be from what they called home, THIS was their home. They were now family. The Sergeant dismissed them, and they took their belonging into the barracks to find a locker and bed.

April chose a lower bunk. She never liked sleeping on a top bunk. She laid her two suitcases on her bed and opened one up. She hung up the sweats and fatigues that were issued to her. She also put her guitar in her locker in its case, it just fit. She then sat on her bed and waited while others filled their lockers with clothing and all sorts of things that they brought with them - including pictures of loved ones, family, or risqué photos of movie stars.

After a half hour or so, another Drill Sergeant came in with two Military Police, MPs. One by one they opened lockers and trashed them completely. They either had too much stuff in them, or the MPs ripped down photos that were taped on their locker doors.

When they got to April's locker there were so few articles of clothing, the Drill Sergeant looked curiously at her. He pointed to the guitar in its case and asked, "What's that?"

April told him it was her guitar as she pulled it out and opened the case to show him. She hoisted the guitar to her waist and began to strum a tune. She chose "Soldier Boy," a song she learned from her Dad years ago. The Drill Sergeant looked at her as if he were mesmerized as he nodded his head with the tune. He touched April on the shoulder, turned, and left.

"Boy, that saying sure is right," one of the guys said. "Music does calm the savage beast," and many in the room began to laugh.

April put her guitar back into its case, then back into the locker. She was glad she had her guitar. It caused no trouble, soothed her at quiet moments, and, in this situation, it saved all their butts.

Soon it was time to do exercises. Jumping jacks and running in place, sit ups, and squats, for two hours straight. Everyone was thirsty and ran for the water except April. She had learned long ago to put a pebble under her tongue to keep her from getting thirsty. She took her time and only a few sips, under the watchful eye of the Sergeant McCoy.

His name was Robert McCoy. He was from Mississippi and was born fourth out of eleven children. They were poor, with nothing to do, and not much to look forward to in the way of education or jobs. He joined the Navy at age eighteen.

He never went back to the south. The Navy was his home, his family. He never married and had no children or girlfriend. He kept to himself. He was a stickler for discipline. You did everything his way. He only told you once, so you had better pay attention.

For some reason, Sergeant Bob McCoy singled out April, not in a bad way, but he kept on her more so than the others. He read her profile and he was impressed. She wanted to push herself when others were content to move out in six weeks. He hoped she would stay on.

One afternoon April made a mistake a small one, but nevertheless that mistake earned April to run around the back of the canteen until Sergeant told her to stop. Everyone went on with their two hours of exercises and then a five-mile run. When they got back, they all showered and went to the mess hall. Then they returned to their appointed rooms for lights out and to go to sleep.

As Sergeant Bob sat there in the canteen, he and another Sergeant heard noises in the rain. It had begun to rain as they came back to the base from their five-mile run. But there was no doubt it sounded like a horse sloshing around in the mud. When all at once it hit him, surely it was not D out there. He thought he told her to stop. He got up and went out to look with the other men and sure enough there she was, still running the square, soaked to her skin, but she kept going.

From the doorway some of the men began to laugh, saying how stupid she was to keep going in the rain when Sergeant Bob told them, "She is not stupid, she is obedient. She did as I ordered, and I admire that in a person. You can bet she is tired, but she didn't complain or quit."

He strode out in the rain adjusting his hat with the plastic covering. "D," he yelled. "D, stop and come in front of me right now," he ordered.

April stopped right in front of him, saluting. She was shaking uncontrollably in the rain. she was soaking wet, her hair, her clothing, her boots, everything on her was soaked. He addressed her, "D, are you tired?"

"No, Sir. I am not tired, Sir," she said.

"I think you have had enough. Next time when I order you to do something, do it right," he barked at her.

"Sir. Yes, Sir," April replied to him. She saluted him, he saluted her, and she was dismissed.

April headed to her room and tip toed as quietly as she could to get dry clothing. She grabbed some energy bars and headed to the showers to get these wet clothing off and get warm. She had to peel off the wet clothing as they stuck to her. She stood in the warmth of the shower water, rubbing her arms, and she began to feel warm. She showered until her skin was red, then quickly dried and dressed. As she put her wet clothing in a bag to wash, she tossed her hair to dry. She went back to her room having already eaten her bars, slipped into bed, and was asleep in two minutes.

The doors were being banged on at 5 a.m. April was sitting on her bunk dressed and waiting. Sergeant Bob entered their barracks and saw her, "Ready for another day?"

"Sir. Yes, Sir," she answered him.

He was not expecting her to be up. He thought she would still be asleep with the workout she had yesterday. He noticed that some were still sleeping, but there she was sitting ready to go. But her eyes told him otherwise. She had bags under her eyes, and they were bloodshot. He admired her spirit, never giving in.

Soon the horns blew for all the recruits to line up for inspection, the day's two-hour exercises, and today there would be a ten-mile run. He knew they would not be expecting that, and he wanted to test the recruits' resolve.

After two hours of grueling sits, squats, and regular exercises, Sergeant Bob whistled for them to keep going in the two lines they were already in for their run. He did not tell them it was for ten long miles.

April was in the middle of the pack. She felt all right, and that she could keep up. At the four-mile mark some were beginning to complain every now and then, but she kept her lips shut tight.

Sergeant Bob watched her from the corner of his eye. She showed no sign of slowing down, no sign of tiredness, and she was not complaining. On they went, Sergeant Bob whistled and ordered them to do it again. There was a lot of groaning, but they kept going. At about the eight-mile mark some had fallen behind, some just could not go anymore, but there was D keeping pace with the front runners. He jogged beside her. "Are you tired, D?" he shouted.

"No, Sir. I am not tired," she said with winded breath.

He laughed and said, "Just checking, just checking," and on they went. At around the ninth mile or a bit more, April had now come to the front of the group. Many others had fallen behind, some had stopped, but she was determined not to. She did not even think about that. She was running the Piney Woods, a run she knew every rock and every tree. She loved that run.

When they reached the barracks, those in the front halted, walked around to cool down, and go for water. April did not.

When Sergeant Bob came to where they were, he eyed D. He was astounded that as a woman she had the stamina to keep going and even surpass those who did not go through what she had the day before. He knew comparing her would cause a problem, but she was a girl, a tough girl, a hardened and obedient one at that.

The weeks went on and each exercise now was with hoses of water drenching them full blast and they were expected to keep going. They crawled through lines of mud, swam in pools with their legs or arms tied, and limited to four hours of sleep each night. It was an adjustment for April. She was used to five hours of sleep, but to lose one hour was not so bad. She was thankful she had a rigorous schedule all her life.

They were taken out on the rifle range to shoot, each one in turn, and their targets were examined. When it was D's turn, she took the rifle like it was a familiar friend, aimed it, held it steady, and shot. She could hit the center mark from three-hundred yards. "Not shabby," the Sergeant commented.

As time went on D was taken out on the shooting range often. At the six-week's training she could swing her rifle up and shoot nailing a target at six-hundred yards, which her Sergeant was impressed.

The most stressful training, but one she adapted to very well, was the course where people would pop out and you had a split second to determine if it was friend or foe. Sergeant Bob was astounded at April's first round. She instinctively dropped, rolled, and was able to ascertain who it was which got her ninety four points. Sergeant Bob was certain April would be good for ops missions.

The First Mission

AT THE END OF THEIR TRAINING SOME WERE ASKED TO VOLUNTEER on missions, and D raised her hand. After conferring with Sergeant Bob, she was then brought before the Commanding Officer of the base. April was given detailed instructions on the mission to see if she would: 1. be able to act under pressure; and 2. to clearly see the outcome for her and the small group of men with her.

The mission was accepted. She met the other three Frogmen she was to accompany and assist in retrieving men held captive for ransom in another country. They had their instructions. They packed light and headed out at 2 a.m. the next morning.

D sat in the plane, there were no words, she felt confident, but did not know the men with her. Finally, she looked at them, and she said, "I will do my best to accomplish the mission at hand and watch that each of you come out all right."

They looked at each other and began to laugh. She sure was confident and had no experience whatsoever, so this ought to be interesting. But they also knew she was needed on this mission. They too would watch over her and make sure she came out all right.

One Frogman leaned forward, "Sister, you can bet we are family," one of them said to her leaning forward to shake her hand, "Hi. I am Mark. This is Brian and T. We are on this mission together. We will stay that way, finish it, and no man left behind."

As they flew on, April realized they were crossing over an ocean. She knew they were heading to the Middle East but did not know which country. She did not know what their mission was exactly, or what she was specifically to do yet!

Mark nudged her and said, "I see your mind is racing. Don't do that. None of us know our mission just yet. This is the time to relax, to rest. We will have complete details of our mission before we land. Everything will be outlined. Keep fresh, don't dwell on what you don't know. You must learn to act, not react. You have been trained to focus."

So, she realized Mark was right, there was no sense trying to make sense when you did not know details. She had been trained to know the difference, so she leaned back and relaxed. She heard the drone of the plane's engines, and she could almost feel the wind. They were flying in the rain or so it seemed. She sat there and began to pray silently, then she felt oddly at peace.

Here she was, about to enter a hostile country and retrieve hostages. It was exciting and heart racing, but she was calm and at peace. She thanked her Heavenly Father for his mercy towards her and prayed that they would all come out safely.

Soon the cockpit door opened and there were papers going into Mark's hands. All the Frogmen leaned forward to hear what was to happen. April learned they were in the Middle East. There were three officers being held for ransom, and they were to extract them. Mark handed her a photo, "Here study this photo. If you see this man, we are to capture him. He is a known terrorist that bombed a military base in Africa. He is here. Imprint his face in your mind."

April studied the photo looking for identifying marks, scars, or misshaped features on his face. She felt confident if she saw him, she would recognize him.

Soon the side door opened, they were over the ocean and would have to swim the three miles to shore. Each of them had a backpack on with dry clothing for this mission. As they jumped, Brian, T, then Mark motioned April to jump. She looked down into a sea of black and stepped off. Mark joined them and each of them swam effortlessly, quietly to the shore.

Once there they were hidden in the dark by rocks and changed into their clothing. April however did not have the military clothing the others had. She had a dress and a large shawl to wear over her arms and face. She understood her mission was to lure the men guarding the hostages out. How she was going to do that was not clear, but she felt her imagination would figure it out.

As the men left to take their positions, they showed April where their men were being held. She purposely walked up the road to be noticed. She leaned over as if she were sick with too much alcohol, and a guard held a rifle at her. She laughed at him, and half bent over as if she were drunk. Mark was shocked, he did not expect this. In no time six men were outside, some had come up to April to "help" her, but their intentions were not to help her at all.

Mark heard her say, "Laa. Laa," and she staggered forward. The men began to laugh, and in no time, there were seven men outside all trying to use this easy prey woman.

While their attention was on her, two of the Frogmen slipped inside the building and untied the hostages. They were on their way out when the terrorist whose face April had studied came up the road to see what was causing the commotion.

April stood up half staggering and calling to him. He approached her and took her to the opposite side of the building, away from his men. He pulled her hair back forcefully, and she let him. From the corner of her eye, April saw the two Frogmen leaving the building where she was to another house close by. She wanted to buy them time to get out.

When they were safely gone, she let the terrorist kiss her roughly. He was beginning to tear her clothing and she stopped him. Then she took her finger and slid it across his face and over his nose to his lips to tease him while she whispered in his ear.

She led him inside and she spied a rope lying on a chair. She had him sit down and she eased him in the chair, sitting on top of his lap. The terrorist was all smiles in anticipation of what she would do next. She took the rope and dangled it across his head and chest all the while crisscrossing the rope until, finally, she tied his hands behind him to the back side of the chair. She began to undress, and the man was all smiles saying, "Yes, yes," in his language. One of his men came in to see where he was, and the terrorist screamed at him to get out. He ordered them to go and drink.

April was praying Mark had been watching her. She knew she had to capture this man, so she untied his hands from the back of the chair and lead him outside to the other building next door. The terrorist thought she did not want them to be interrupted again and went willingly.

As April lured the man, she saw a tiny flash of light which she knew was Mark. With one huge swing of her arms, she hit the side of the terrorist's face knocking him out cold. The terrorist laid there at the side of the building and Mark scampered over, crouched down.

"Okay, great job. Now help me. You go on that side." With each one of them holding his arms, they drug and carried the man from the house to the rocks. They gathered their packs and began to swim out. There was not one shot fired. The terrorist's men were getting drunk and thought their boss was with the woman.

As the three swam towards their pickup point, the man awoke. He breathed deeply and was about to scream when April sucker punched him in the head, knocking him out cold again. Mark laughed at her. As they reached their pickup point, they got out of the water and looked around. There was no one around so they waited in the dark, quietly. No one spoke. They just sat there waiting.

Soon they heard the sound of a chopper, and sure enough it broke through the trees and hovered. They hurried to the chopper. T and Brian were dragging the terrorist, and the other three hostages climbed aboard as well as Mark and April. When they were all in the chopper it lifted off. The terrorist was awake again and spit toward April. She got up and tightened his ropes until he could not move at all. Then she pulled a sock out of her pocket and shoved it into his mouth. "I had enough of him already," she said.

The Frogmen were impressed, she certainly had done her job well. They had extracted the hostages without one shot being fired, she easily lured the man they had been looking for, and no one saw them. So, no one would know.

April sat there half dressed, wet in a ripped dress trying to cover up. She had been able to swim, no problem, but she felt so exposed on the plane with six men. Brian saw her discomfort and threw her a jacket to cover herself. She took it and put it on.

The other two Frogmen were trying to assist the three hostages they had recovered. It was obvious they had been drugged, beaten, and the three refused to talk. That was understandable.

As they flew April felt that rush of adrenalin subsided, it left her feeling tired. She pulled her legs up to her chest and soon was drifting off to sleep. When her head fell back in a jerk she woke up and looked around. Most were sleeping, but not the three men who had come along with her on the mission. Brian, Mark, and T were awake like hawks.

"If you are tired rest," Mark told her. "We will be back on base in about two hours."

"I would rather get to know you guys," she said, and the three of them looked at each other.

"Well, you know my name is Mark. I am married to a beautiful woman and have two children, one boy and a girl. I live in Maryland. I have several hobbies including racing cars, hunting, and my kids."

"T" here I am not married, no kids. I live the life I want, and my passions are fast cars, flying, and sail boating. I live in Texas."

"Brian," nodding his head towards her. "I am married for a year now, no kids. We both like body building, running, and rock climbing. I live in Utah."

Then it was her turn, "I am April. I have 2 Moms and 1 Dad. One is my birth Mom. My other Mom is married to my Dad. They adopted me. I have raced at the Triple Crown and won with the only male I have ever trusted," and they laughed at her. "I also raise cattle and I thrive on competition, much to the disappointment of everyone around me. I came here because I felt I needed to come, as if it were calling me."

"Oh, she's frog material all right," T said. "That calling just won't let you go." They all laughed again.

From that time forward, April felt comfortable with these guys. They all respected her and trusted her as much as she did them. They all worked well together on the missions they subsequently assigned.

Sergeant Bob could not have been prouder. He boasted about the one who he ran in the mud, but who came out smelling like a rose. No matter the mission she did her best. The guys liked and respected her. She was one of them. As he told her on her first day, here they were family, and he was right.

They were all family but one. There was a Sergeant that did not like April at all. His name was Carl. He felt she was a bit of a showoff, privileged, came from money. Sooner or later she would be in his pen, and he would show her what a man was made of. April did not know, but in time she would find out. It would be one of her greatest challenges.

Africa, I Am On My Way,

THE MISSIONS CAME AND WENT. THEY WERE ALL SIMILAR, dangerous, get in, do your job, get out as quickly as you can. She never felt afraid, her instincts were honed. When she was busy, time seemed to fly by, the months passed. Each day had been crossed out in red on her calendar.

One mission was open, and it interested April. It was for protection at a military base in Africa. She had always wanted to go to Africa, and now was her chance. April notified her superior officer she wanted to go on the mission. She was asked to train hard in hot weather to get conditioned. April did much of the same routine Jinks had taught her when she was training for the Winter Olympics, to be strong in body and mind. In two weeks April was ready.

April shipped out alone, but there were men on the base for support. They touched down in eleven hours. She was out of the plane with papers in hand for the Captain of this base. The air was hot and humid, and she liked it. April found where her assigned bunk would be. After settling in, she spoke with the Commander of the mission.

There were villages that the military were protecting from having their people shot or their villages destroyed. There was a pesky sniper that had hit six of the soldiers so far, killing one. This had to stop. At every exit or entry to the compound the sniper would be shooting at them, and they could not find him.

April decided that the next day would be her chance. She asked to be dismissed and went to her bunk, she knelt down, and asked her Heavenly Father for help.

There is no joy in killing. The soldiers were here protecting the villagers so they could continue their lives in a normal way. They wanted to prevent the militants from coming to take women and children to torture them and kill the men. That was wrong, and April asked for the gift of the Holy Ghost to be ever present and strong with her on the day she would go out. She needed protection, for insight, and help in what to do. She reaffirmed that her life was his. She wanted to be peaceful, but, if necessary, to take out the assailant that would want to kill her or the people.

She went to bed feeling comforted. She did not have stress or worry. Early the next morning April knew what she was to do. She had had a dream, and in that dream, it was revealed to her what she was to do. April asked for a villager's dress to cover herself. She also had a long-sleeved black shirt to cover her arms, chest, and neck. With a head covering no one could guess she was a white person with blonde hair.

She briefly told the two men who were going with her what her plans were. but just briefly. She knew if she were to tell them in detail, they would think she was crazy.

"We are going to walk to that field. As we enter it, I want both of you to stay down low in the tall grass, do not move, and do not make a sound. You WILL see me, and you will not fully understand. I know this sounds crazy to you, but I am depending on God to help me. You must trust what I say." She did not stick around to hear their answer.

April walked through the tall grass praying mightily. Her hands brushed over the tall grass, and she began to call out as in a loud song. She was calling the kings in to her, the kings of the Serengeti to come and she heard their roars. They slowly came in a large pride of thirty or more, and they roared at her. April motioned with her arms in a stay motion, as if saying. "Down, down," and the lions and lionesses did just that. Some snarled at her, but they stayed lying down.

"Do you believe this?" The one man asked the other.

"Nope. I am not sure I am seeing this," the other answered.

Now the militant sniper was watching all of this, and he thought April was a witch. He did not want bad luck and did not want to harm her. He watched her disappear in the brush and trees. He had never seen anything like that. He shook his head and shoulders and set about to sight in his next target.

During that time, April began to climb a tree. It was difficult with the dress on, and the rifle slung on her shoulder. It took her a good four to five minutes to make it to the top of the tree. As she sat there, she looked through her scope. She saw the rim of the sniper's sight. It glistened in the last light and new moon. She panned around and saw four more, two in the grass and two more in trees. So, she thought to herself, there was not one, but five of them.

Carefully she aimed at the militant sniper in the tree who had not seen her. She panned again to be sure where her targets were. And as if you counted: 1, 2, 3, 4, 5, it was over. That quickly, that effortlessly. The only noise was the zing of the bullets through the air, one after another. As she climbed down, she motioned with her arms in a sweeping motion to the kings, and the pride had their dinner.

She walked out to where she had left the two men. As she came, they stood up. "Okay, I guess that's it for a while. You two all right? April asked them.

"Ugh, yeah," one said in a sarcastic way, "Can you explain how you called those lions in and how you managed this?"

"Sure," she said. "By the power of the Holy Ghost. If you want to know, I need a couple of days to teach you, but I think I ship out tomorrow," April said. She was grateful that she was living and worthy to have the Holy Ghost for his protection and guidance. She left them a card, *Articles of Faith*, and a telephone number.

On another mission that April was part of but did not go out on. She was affected deeply and unexpected, they had lost a brother.

They had been on a retrieve mission, and he was hit in the back. The bullet penetrated through his back to his heart. Mac was dead before he knew it. He was a good man, a great man who never gave up or would consider quitting or letting someone behind.

The entire group was stunned and hurting. There was no religious priest or chaplain on their small base. There was no one, but her. April knew what to do. She had been to several funerals in her lifetime. She knew this was necessary for the men he had served with for comfort and closure.

April got some help from some of the guys. They made a makeshift room with chairs, they opened tents to make walls, and found a piano that was missing several keys, but it would do. Mac's boots were put up on a wooden box with his dog tags laying on them. As the men filed in, April began to play the piano. She played the song "Let it be" by the Beatles. It was Mac's favorite song and very appropriate for his funeral service here on this outpost.

She began to sing softly as she played, and as the men sat there many were crying.

After the song, April walked to the front of the room and invited anyone who wanted to come forward to say a few words about their friend Mac to come up. No one moved, so April began to say a few words. "I did not know Mac as well as many of you, but what I do know, Mac was one heaven of a man. He was dependable, honest, and never gave up." She then told them a joke Mac had shared with her one day out in the field. April told them that it may not be customary to laugh at a funeral, but knowing Mac, he would. "I am not being disrespectful, so here goes," she said.

There was a Baptist minister and a huge congregation singing hymns at a river's edge. Many were being baptized when the minister noticed a drunken man stumble out of the woods. The minister called to the man, "Brother, brother, come to me," and the man did with his whiskey jug on his shoulder. "Now, brother, tell me, have you found Jesus?" And with that the minister dunked the man under the water for 30 seconds.

He pulled the man up by his collar and belt and asked him again. "Tell me, brother, have you found Jesus?"

The man answered, "No, I ain't."

Down under the water again, this time for a full minute. Then the minister pulled him up by his collar and belt, and hollered at his soaking wet head, "Now, brother, have you found Jesus?"

The man hollered back "No, I ain't!"

By now the minster was beside himself. He was disgusted at the man's drunkenness, his ignorance, and refusal to accept Jesus Christ. So, with all his strength, the minister dunked the man and held him under the water for a full two minutes. Pulling the sputtering man out of the water who was gasping for air, the minister screamed at the man, "NOW, BROTHER, I ASK YOU. HAVE YOU FOUND JESUS?!?! The man trying to catch his breath said, "Are you sure he went in right here?"

The men laughed, "Now it is time for you all to come up and say a few words about how you knew Mac and what you did with him. The time is now yours," she said.

One got up, he was brief, and then another, and another. Some would join one who was up front, they would hug and cry. An hour or so later there many were still getting up telling jokes they had shared or talking about the brotherhood they had shared.

The wake lasted over two hours. It was a wonderful way for Mac's friends to heal, find closure, and solidify their brotherhood. At the end, April went to the front again. She wanted to share a story with the men. She said, "I read this a while back".

A man who was deathly sick, got the final diagnosis. It was confirmed he had cancer and only three months to live.

He looked at the doctor and said, "Tell me what it's like on the other side."

"I don't know." the doctor replied.

The man was taken back and said, "You are a Christian. How can you say you don't know?"

Right then there was a noise on the other side of the door, whining and scratching. "Do you hear that?" The doctor said to the man. "That is my dog. He has never been in this office before or this room, but he hears my voice." The doctor opened the door, and the dog came bounding in jumping up to his master. "I believe, when it is my turn, I will go willingly with joy because I know my Master is there on the other side."

Later when the Captain, who had been called away just before Mac's passing, returned and learned what had happened to Mac.

He was told about the wonderful service that was given to him by the crew, and the Captain was grateful.

He made a trip to see Lt. D. and April assured the Captain that everything was done to strengthen the morale of the men, to solidify Mac's spirit with theirs. To them, Mac was not gone, his spirit tarried with each of them.

The Captain put his hands on April's shoulders, with his head down, and he thanked her.

April just humbly said, "It was an honor to serve with this unit. I am glad I was here to be part of all of it." It was one of the most difficult missions she had served on, and she would never forget it, the men or Mac.

April Goes on Leave

FAST FORWARD TO ONE YEAR LATER. APRIL GOT LEAVE TO GO HOME for six weeks. She was anxious to go and also a bit nervous. She had cut her long hair. It was now just a bob. She wondered if her parents would recognize her. She was very tanned, v dark brown.

She caught her flight from Florida to California and arrived home in the middle of the afternoon. It was Friday so she guessed as usual her Mom would be grocery shopping in town. She walked along from the bus station, the very same one she arrived at thirteen years earlier. Things had not changed much, and she was glad to see that. As she walked, a pickup truck came along and slowed down, it was the John and Betty. They stopped and said they almost did not recognize her, and asked if she wanted a ride.

She did, so she threw her bag in the back of the truck and climbed aboard. As they rode through town, her hair was blowing in the wind. She saw the town as she remembered it. They slowed down at the grocery store and as they stopped Miranda Di Angelo went driving right past them, and never noticed them.

April told John and Betty it was all right. She would catch up with her soon. She got her bag and waving to them began to walk. It did not take long for friends to see her. Two cars slowed down, stopped, and they got out and hugged her. They were all excited to see her and she them.

While they stood there, Amber who she had known in High School but was not very close with, but whom she liked, told her that tonight was the chicken dinner at the fire hall.

"Your Mom and Dad will both be there. It would be awesome to surprise them there," and they all agreed.

So, she headed out with them in their car and stayed briefly with Amber and her family until it was time to leave for the dinner. She had a quick shower, dressed in full military dress, and headed out, asking them to not say one word that she was home.

At the fire hall she stowed her bag beside the refrigerator. She saw lines of people go in the front door. Either they purchased tickets or turned over their pre-purchased tickets. April saw many people she knew, Sam and Elaine Marshall, and others. Finally, her parents pulled into the parking lot. Dad looked tired and Mom was chatting away as usual. April laughed to herself, and she felt her eyes tearing up. She had missed them immensely, but for sanity's sake she kept them out of her mind.

She waited another half hour or so and went into the fire hall through the back door. She was greeted, hugged and re-hugged. Someone went out to see where her parents were and called her over to show her.

The dinners were taken to the guests. So as the servers brought out the dinners, April was to take her Mom's meal to her, and the surprise would be known. But she had to wait until they reached that spot at the tables. Dishes full of food went past her on carts, one after another. Then April was tapped to follow, the cart was lined up behind April's parents so they would not see her. As the plates were set in front of the patrons, April leaned over and put her Mother's dinner in front of her and said, "Here is your dinner, Mom. Hope you enjoy it."

Miranda heard "that" voice and the "Mom" was a dead giveaway. She looked up and began to scream. She could not believe her eyes. She stood, hugged her daughter, and was crying.

Her father stood up and hugged them both while the entire room of people began to clap. It was a good homecoming surprise, and it took some time for everyone to settle down. Many came to April to say "hello" or congratulate her. Her Mom held on to a piece of her clothing, not so she could not walk away, but for Miranda it was not real yet. She wanted to hold on to her until it sunk in, her daughter was home.

April sat with her parents, but due to the emotional stress she could not eat, or rather she preferred not to eat. She loved seeing all the familiar faces, and before long Elaine Marshall came to her. April stood and hugged her as if she were like her Mom. Her eyes filled with tears and the two of them stood there for quite some time. "Forgive me," April asked of her.

"Oh, no. It's quite all right. I am so glad you have a chance to come home. I really want to talk with you sometime while you are home, so do please call me when you can," then she left to sit with her husband.

Gordon Di Angelo's eyes met with his daughter's. It was obvious he had much to say, but this was not the time. April winked at him to let him know it was all right. Miranda kept staring at her daughter, "You know we really should stop and see June and Lena," she said. They will be thrilled."

Gordon nodded his head in agreement, "Well, then we can't dawdle here all night," he said. Miranda shooed her napkin at him.

Within an hour or so, the Di Angelos stood up to leave. Gordon shook the hand of the Wilsons sitting next to him, when all at once the crowd broke into a song, *America*. They must have scrambled to find a trumpet player, a drummer, and someone to play the piano. They did a fine job, really.

The people all stood up with their hands across their hearts singing, and it was truly beautiful. April felt so humble and close to tears, she did her best to keep them back. As the Di Angelo family walked out, there were shouts of "Welcome Home", "Welcome Back", and others who whistled and called her by name.

Outside April felt hot, so she took off her jacket. She walked with her parents to her Dad's truck. "How is it running for you, Dad? Any problems?"

"No, no not at all. This truck is so dependable and good on gas, it surprised me. I have not had it in the shop once. Well, for inspection and to change the fluids and oil, but that was it. It's a great truck really!"

April was glad it was the one thing she gave her Dad that was just for him.

They got in the truck and headed for town. As they came to Third Street, where June and Lena lived, Dad pulled into the back alley. "Often if they are not home, the car is gone," he said, but sure enough their car was in their garage. Her parents walked in front of her, up the walk to the side door and Gordon knocked. "Is anyone home?"

"Just a minute. Just one minute," a voice said, it was Lena.

"Is Nora here too?" Gordon asked.

"Yes, she is in the living room. Come on in. Come in," she said.

"Well, we brought along someone who wanted to see you both," Gordon said.

April followed along last in the line. As her Mom and Dad stepped to the side revealing April, both women jumped up and ran to her.

April found herself covered in hugs and kisses. The women both had tears of joy and laughed and cried at the same time. Miranda began to cry too, there was no denying that the three of them were Mothers to April, they all loved her.

The women urged everyone to sit down. Lena went to the kitchen for iced tea and sodas. They wanted to know everything: what she did, what it was like, the countries she had been in, and what she did there. To spare them from worrying, April told them basic things like exercises and running. She did not mention sharp shooting. She told them about some of the countries, looking for things, but not people. She did not mention the lives taken to accomplish the mission.

All the women were so happy. Nora touched her bobbed hair. "I know," April said. "It will grow back," and they all smiled.

"Oh, nothing for me to eat," both Gordon and Miranda protested.

April sat there smiling while munching on pretzels. She could not count how many times her Mother had told her that when she was in a home and offered food, to eat it. It would be rude not to. So, she had it over her Mom on this one.

Before they knew it the clock stuck 10:00 p.m. "Oh, Dear, we really must go, but I am sure we can get together this week, maybe for dinner?" Miranda asked the women, and both agreed.

"How long will you be home?" Nora asked April.

"I have three weeks, unless they call me back for some reason," she answered them.

"Oh," came out of all of their mouths, including her Dad's.

"It's not so bad," April reassured them, "It is like college in a way, but I came home sooner." They shook their heads, but April was not sure what that meant, yes or no.

Dad was first out the door. April had a difficult time leaving Lena and Nora. Both the older women hugged her as if it were her last day on earth. Soon they were in the truck again heading for home. Dad stopped at the front walk and April got out and just stared at the walk. "What's wrong?" Miranda asked her.

"Nothing I just never realized how great it is to walk on this path again," she said.

Soon inside and Ruby who had aged some was dancing and jumping to greet her. April swooped her up to her face and she licked her over and over. She sat in the living room holding Ruby. She rolled on her back and would not leave her. "You should go to bed, Sweetie," her Mom said to her as she headed up the stairs.

"I am coming. I had to spend some time with my ole' buddy." April headed up the steps carrying Ruby. She undressed and crawled into her old bed. The sheets were fresh. They smelled so good. Mom must have hung them out on the line to dry. Ruby was at her side, and it was like old times. April heard her Dad snoring, and then her Mom too. Yup just like before she left and as April laid in bed, she felt overwhelming gratitude. So much so that she began to cry. She slipped out of bed on her knees and offered a prayer of thanks. She got back into bed and was asleep in less than five minutes.

April woke up with Ruby licking her face. It startled her. She was not sure where she was for a moment. "Oh, Ruby, you stinker," she said. She got out of bed looking at the clock on her nightstand. "8:00 a.m. that can't be," she said out loud. She pulled up the shade on her window and sure enough the sun was bright out. She had not slept that long ever.

She skipped down the stairs, and Mom was in the living room reading the Saturday paper. "Did Dad leave already?" she asked her Mom.

"Oh, yes. It's late, Dear. He left about 6 a.m. this morning, you were over tired I guess," Mom said.

"It was the time change too," April said.

April flopped down on the couch, pulling Ruby up beside her. "Don't you want breakfast?" her Mom asked her.

"What's good?" April asked back. Her Mom threw a small pillow at her and both of them laughed. April got up and there were waffles still on a plate, she popped one in the toaster to warm it up, put it on a paper plate, and came back into the living room. "Mom what are the plans for the week? Do you know? You said you wanted to make dinner for June and Nora to come over."

"Yes, I do. That would be nice for all of us. Don't you think so?" her Mom asked her.

"Yes, but I also want to see Mrs. Marshall and there are a few places I want to go to for about a week," April told her.

"Where do you want to go?" her Mother asked.

"Well, I want to see a few people I have not seen for over fourteen years. Like Barb Cunningham, the woman who was so kind to me on the bus. And Johnnie if I can find him. He was the bus driver. And I hope to see how the Nuns are doing. You know with the new building and all. I hope it all worked out well for them. I never went back after that race," April said to her.

"So, then you won't be here for the whole time?" Her Mom asked her.

"No, I think it is time, past time, I see some of the people who brought me here. And I know that you want to have Poppo and the family here too, and I love that idea. I just need a week away to top off the bucket list that has been sitting idle for so many years," April said.

Her Mom looked hurt, disappointed. So, April got up and knelt before her Mother's legs and told her that this was nothing. She would have her for fifteen days when the long-awaited visits were over. Miranda touched her daughter's face. She was always trying to help others, showing kindness to others, and that would never stop.

She knew her daughter loved her and her husband, and she also knew if it were her, she would do the same thing. "Of course, you go. I understand. I will plan for the family to come, but I think you really should see Mrs. Marshall before you go," Miranda said.

"Okay. She leaned up and kissed her Mom's cheek then she got up to call Mrs. Marshall who answered the telephone on the second ring.

"Hello?"

"Hello, Mrs. Marshall. How are you. This is April."

"Oh, April. At first, I did not know who was calling me. Yes, of course. I am fine. What have you been up to so far today?"

"Well, not much. I slept in till 8:00 a.m."

"What? You slept in?" they both laughed.

"I am trying to organize some visits with friends from over the years, and Mom wants to plan some things with me. The next two weeks are going to fly by. That said, I want to see you before I leave. Is that possible?"

"Oh, sure it is. Yes, come anytime. It is just me here at home now. My husband is at work all day."

"Okay then, how about tomorrow. I can meet you someplace, or . . ."

Mrs. Marshall interrupted April, "Just come up to the house. Really, it's all right."

"Okay then, see you tomorrow. Say about 8 a.m.?" April asked.

"Say about 9," Mrs. Marshall said, and laughed.

Miranda heard the conversation and was glad. No one said anything to April and Miranda felt if anything was said, it should come from the Marshalls.

The next day there was a whopping breakfast, April wondered who was coming. On the table were stacks of blueberry pancakes, bacon, a small sausage on a plate, home fried potatoes, juice, and toast.

"Sit and eat," Miranda said hustling back into the kitchen.

"Mom who is coming over for breakfast?" April asked her Mom, eyeing the clock on the wall. It was 7:02 in the morning and here was a spread for a small army.

"Why, no one. Your Dad has already eaten, and the rest is for you."

April was aghast, there was no way she could eat all this, not even a plateful. April sat down taking a blueberry muffin that smelled so good, she put a slice of bacon on her plate and a tablespoon full of home fries.

"Is that all you are going to eat?" her Mother asked her.

"Mom, I never ate that much when I was at home. Do you think the Navy turned me into an eating machine?" she asked her Mother.

Miranda began to put the food away. "Warmups are always good, and breakfast can be for dinner too," she said. And then the telephone rang, "Hello." Miranda answered the call.

"Hello. Oh, Miranda, this is Elaine Marshall. Has April left yet?"

"No, she has not. She is right here."

"Okay, ask her if she can wait until 9:15 or so to come. All right? I have my hands full right now," Elaine said.

"Okay, I will tell her. You take care," with that Miranda hung up the telephone.

"Did you hear?" she asked April.

"Yes, I did. Good thing she called, or I would have left," April said. So, she helped her Mother clean up, did the dishes, then April kissed her Mother and left.

The drive to the Marshall's was a bit unnerving. It made April's stomach queasy, all because of Hugh. She pulled the car into the driveway and at the bottom of the garage got out, closed the car door, and headed to the steps to go to their home. She was going to knock, but Elaine was there at the door to greet her. "Come on in," Elaine said. "How are you?"

"I am all right. I wanted to see you before I left" April said.

"Leaving? Where are you going? I mean, you are not going back to duty this soon, are you?" Elaine asked April. "No, no nothing like that. I have a bucket list to fulfill, and I must get them done. I want to see people who have helped me to this point in my life, some from far in my past," April told her.

"Come on into the living room," Elaine said to April. They sat down and Elaine said to April. "You look very uncomfortable, so I guess we better talk this out. April, Hugh has made some big strides in his life. He has . . ."

April interrupted her. "Excuse me, but I did not come here to talk about Hugh. Part of the reason I went into the Frogman program was because of Hugh. I was angry. I guess I still am. I do not want Hugh Marshall in my life. Hugh made that choice a long time ago for me." April felt like she was bristling.

Elaine got up and handed April a photo of a toddler sitting up-right on the Marshall's living room floor. April stared at Elaine with questions in her eyes. "That is Michael. He is one year old now, starting to walk, trying to get into everything, and he looks just like his daddy," Elaine said.

April did not understand, when she left the Marshalls did not want their son near them. He and his girl were not permitting in the Marshall home. "Excuse me, but I am a bit confused," April said.

Elaine began to explain, "Hugh's eyes were opened about the fifth month of pregnancy. Sandra did not want to live on base. She wanted to come home. She was caught in Caruthers with another man, in his home, and they were not having lunch together. Hugh about lost it. He brought her back to the base and gave her "orders" never to do that again."

"He begged his Dad for help and his Dad gave Hugh the number of our attorney. The baby was born in late December, a bit early. He had no complications, but Sandra had no interest in the little guy. As soon as Sandra was released from the hospital, she did not want to stay with Hugh. She packed up some of her clothing and the baby and was headed to Caruthers again."

"Hugh caught her as she was packing up the car, his car. As she was closing the trunk, Hugh released the safety strap that held the baby's seat in the car, lifting out the seat with the baby. Sandra tried to push Hugh and take the baby from him. He told her the baby was his, and if she wanted to leave to just go, and she did."

"We saw a very humble Hugh come to our driveway carrying the baby with him in the car seat. Hugh explained he had to return to active duty, and he could not take the baby with him. It was hard on us, but we asked Hugh what he was going to do about Sandra, and he said it was over. The baby was his, he would raise him when he was out of the service, and if we would help him. One look at the little one and I was hooked. It was not the baby's fault that the Mother was not decent. So, the baby has been with us since he was four weeks old. Hugh does stay with us when he is on leave. In fact, that is why I asked for you to come a half hour later, he just left to go back, and I did not want the two of you running into one another."

"Baby Michael is in the back room taking a nap, would you like to see him?" she asked April. Truth is, April did not want to see the baby. She did not want any part of Hugh, his son, or the drama attached, but there she was following Elaine out of respect into the back room.

When they got to the door Elaine opened the door very slowly not to make noise, and there the baby was asleep in a crib, looking so peaceful like a tiny angel. He melted a part of April's heart. She could not hold this little one accountable for his Daddy's choices.

"Isn't he beautiful?" Elaine questioned.

"He is," April answered. The baby began to move his mouth as if he were about to speak, and his eyes, although closed, were moving about as if he were seeing something they could not. Elaine motioned for April to follow her out of the baby's room.

They went back into the living room and continued. "So that is what I do now, and I am fulfilled," Elaine said. "I thought of you and how I could tell you, and I just hope you are not upset with me," she asked of April.

"Upset with you? Why would I be? I mean you set Hugh straight and are taking care of your grandson while he is away," April said. "You have what you wanted most, your sons and a grandson in close contact with you."

"Hugh is headed back for orders. I do not know where. Maybe the two of you will end up working together and resolve your differences. I pray for it every day," Elaine said.

April felt her arms bristle, "I respect you immensely, but I am not interested in Hugh. I don't think I could ever trust him again. He hurt me, showed no care, no consideration for me whatsoever, so I hope we don't meet. He can have his life and me mine," April said. "I was not the one who inflicted the pain, or started any of this, Hugh was. For that reason, I would never reconsider. It's over."

Elaine sat there in disbelief and said, "April forgiveness is a wonderful and necessary thing. I hope even if only to forgive, the two of you will meet and work together again. It is wrong to hate."

"I don't hate Hugh. I hated what he DID to me. He used me. He could have called or wrote saying I had a change of mind. But no, he was a coward, needing her with him to tell me. He did not have the strength or fortitude to tell me on his own. I do not like people like that. If they can't be open and honest with me, forget it!" April was fueled she did not want to talk about Hugh.

Elaine continued, "April, I remember how hurt you were, and I was in complete agreement with you, but Hugh has changed. He is humble. He is like the old Hugh that we loved. He made a mistake. I have forgiven him, and that baby is not a mistake."

April stood up, she had no more words, "I am thrilled for you, really I am, but I am not interested in Hugh or the baby. I hope to make a life of my own with someone who loves me for who I am. For the qualities, strengths, and weakness I have, and for us to grow together. I would hate to be with someone and feel I had to check his cell phone or where he was all the time in fear of him cheating. I will never live like that. There has to be someone out there for me that I can trust implicitly, as he trusts me. I would never cheat, and I expect that from my man."

"Truly, I love you, Elaine, and Sam and Trevor, but for Hugh. I have forgiven him for what he did, but I will not allow him free reign in my head. I have better things to do than dwell on him. I no longer think about him. I cannot and will never trust Hugh again, not ever."

She stepped forward, hugged Elaine, kissed her cheek, and said, "I hope to see you again before I leave to go back." April squeezed Elaine's hand and let herself out of the door, closing it behind her.

Elaine Marshall sat there with mixed emotions, and she began to cry. She loved that girl so much. She had prayed and prayed for healing in her family. She knew her son caused much pain for April, and she hoped the year away would have healed her, but she was as angry as she was when she left. She felt it would be necessary for Hugh to ask April for forgiveness. It was the building block they both needed to get past all this. She also knew Hugh was empty inside, and as much as he hurt, he would not allow his pride to ask April for forgiveness. Hugh was an officer now. He had missions to go on and his first and foremost thoughts were for his son. Elaine knew that Hugh still had strong feelings for April. So, she would continue to pray that both would humble themselves and have their hearts softened so that one day they both could heal. Maybe they would never be together again, but for both their sakes they both had to forgive and let go.

Elaine knew neither had, so she would continue to take her concerns to the Lord in prayer. She had faith that one day they both would put this behind them.

April drove home with anger in her heart. She wanted to feel indifferent about that baby boy, but part of her melted. That baby was not part of her neither was Hugh's anger or problem, that baby was the innocent one. She knew she had to pray, it was not right to have hate in her heart and anger. If you add the letter D to anger, you have danger.

She pulled into her home driveway and went inside her house, no one was home, everything was cleaned up, Mom was gone. It was a good time for her to take her concerns to a quiet place and give them over to the Lord.

She took the telephone receiver off the hook and laid it down beside the telephone. She locked the door, she made every effort to not have any thing interfere with the concerns she wanted to take to her Heavenly Father, she did not want interrupted in any way, this was important.

April felt Ruby by her leg as she knelt to pray, she patted her head and began:

Dear Father in Heaven,

I humbly ask you hear my prayer, my concerns, in the name of Jesus Christ. Father, I am angry, and I have no right to be. What's past is in the past. Help me, Father, to forgive, to move on, and should any of the past come present in my life, to let it go, to not feel anger, or any negative thoughts. I am ashamed of my actions, Lord. Give me strength to apologize to Elaine and show her I am not angry. Help me, Father, for I am weak. Help me be a better person and strive to live as your son did. Help me learn by his example.

I walk a fine line, Father. A month ago, I was taking lives under the orders of our US Government, which I know I am not responsible for when it is the law of our country. For that I am grateful, and I ask for mercy. It was my job. I take no pleasure in taking lives, my only thought is to rid the world of evil and let you make that judgment. Father, I love thee and I ask with all that I am for your help, to give healing, and to mend wounds.

To show love at all times at all costs, help me, Father, to have peace in my heart, to be strong and merciful, and to be what you want me to be.

I have felt the strongest impressions before I entered the military, Father, that I was supposed to go, as I still do. I do not know why or what it means, but I trust you, Father, and I know as I do, you will lead me to where I am to go. I will continue to trust thee, Father, and know that thy spirit of the Holy Ghost will tarry with me so long as I live worthily. He will guide and direct when I listen. I hope to do all that thou asks of me. I am not afraid, I am willing. No matter should I live or die, Father in Heaven, I serve thee.

For this purpose, I need peace in my heart, Father. I should not have anger, so help me I plead with thee, Father in Heaven. Help me put this anger away from me, fill my soul with gratitude, with happiness, and the steady even flow of love. I can and will do all thou asks of me, with peace in my heart. Thou are great and merciful, wise and kind, know that I love thee, Father and I say this in the name of our Savior, our Redeemer, our Savior, Jesus Christ, Amen.

April leaned over a bit to ruffle Ruby's ears, "I did not hear you say 'Amen', Ruby," and she let out a bark which made April smile.

She carried Ruby upstairs to pack. She pulled out her old travel bag, put in several pairs of pants, shirts, under clothing, socks, and one pair of shoes. She rarely wore make up, but she threw in a few things. April pulled out the only earrings she adored. It was a pair of one carat diamond earrings that was given to her when she was twelve. She put them in an envelope and decided she would wear them if she went out.

That was it. She took her bag downstairs in one hand and Ruby in the other and placed her bag behind the living room door. She opened the door to go to the barn where there were a dozen or so ponies, including Native Son's Momma. That mare was obviously pregnant again, and April wondered if this was another baby Manny had plans for.

She took out the four-wheeler and headed to the Adams' place to see how the milking was going. When she got there Mrs. Adams got so excited that April encouraged her to sit down. April realized quickly how much this woman really did care for her. Mrs. Adams was out of breath and began to speak, "Did you know that my Grandson came back? Oh, I was so thrilled, so happy."

"No. I did not know that. I am glad, though I always thought a lot of him. If he could only get away from his parents, I felt he had a chance," April said.

"Yes. He is milking here, and he started to date Beth. Can you believe that? She is such a nice girl, being a nurse and all. Her Mother likes Brock a lot, so it has been so wonderful. I wish you could have been here to see it all. It was a miracle I tell you, a miracle."

April never doubted it. The two of them sat there for a while and April told her she just wanted to walk out to the barn for a bit. She went out and it was so serene and quiet, nothing like the life she had spent in the last year. She heard the crickets chirping, the birds, and the song the little stream made as the water ran along the field line. That was it.

April walked into the barn and the cows were all inside. The smell took her back, way back to the days when this all began. She walked along and marveled how clean the barn was, what good condition the cows were in, and how clean the milk parlor was with no clutter.

It struck her. They did not need her! The plans were so carefully made and easy to follow, anyone could do this if they just followed the directions. And it put her at ease. She knew that if this farm was run like all the others, everything was happening just as she envisioned. She washed her hands at the parlor sink and went back to see Mrs. Adams. They talked briefly and then April left to head into town to visit Mr. Stevens.

April knocked on the door and heard his cheery, "Come in."

She stepped in and he had been looking in ledgers. When he looked up and saw her, he jumped up and hurried to give her a huge hug. "Oh, my goodness, just look at you all grown up. Here let me make a space for you to sit down."

April was tickled at how he fussed over her. "How are you?" he asked her.

"I am good. Just home for a bit," she said.

"I see. I see," Mr. Stevens said.

"So how are things going for D Farms?" April asked him.

"Well, I have to say even with the milk prices going down, we are doing okay. Better than I expected," he said. D Farms are now up to 782 farms and going strong. We have the highest graduation percentage of any company. I have been so amazed and so humbled by this vision you had. What a wonderful blessing it has been to so many, including me," Mr. Stevens said.

April could not have been happier. She never wanted to make billions of dollars. Her view was to end hunger in America, and to help those who could not afford college.

They sat there together for a while and then April said she had to go. She wanted to be home when her Mom got home. She wanted to make a few more stops.

Mr. Stevens stood up and hugged her. He told April his wife had written to her, but the letter was returned.

"I never know where I will be," she told him. She then wrote down an address for the base.

"Send it to this address and I will get it eventually and I am sorry truly. I didn't know." They said their farewells and then she left.

She drove to town, parking in front of the courthouse. April walked up the steps to the scanners and there were Rusty and Monte. They were so excited to see her that they forgot to ask her to empty her pockets into the tray and go through the scanner. April knew what to do. She went through the required routine without being asked.

She headed to the Judge's chambers. She knocked on the door, but no one answered. She turned the doorknob and walked in. She saw Missy on the telephone talking to someone. Missy looked up and waved for April to come in.

Within minutes the call ended, and Missy stood and ran to April enveloping her in a huge bear hug. "Oh gosh, it's so good to see you," Missy said. How long are you in town?"

"I am just spending today, and then I am leaving for two weeks to catch up with a few other folks that I have not seen in years."

"Oh, that sounds like fun," Missy said to April. "You do want to see the judge, don't you?" Missy asked.

"Yes, if he is here, but if he is tied up in court for a long time, I will catch up with him when I get back," April told her.

"No, just wait about 10 minutes. He is almost finished," Missy said.

So, the two of them sat down and talked, catching up on things in town, the people, who got married, and who was dating whom. "You heard about Hugh, didn't you?" Missy asked April.

"Yes, I heard, but I am no longer interested. I have moved on," April answered her. And then the chamber door opened and in walked Judge Du Val.

"Hey, ho, ho, ho, look who is here," he said excitedly. He came over to April and hugged her for a long time. "Gosh it's so good to see you again. Come with me and tell me all about your year away," and he led her to his chambers.

"I can't stay too long. I have to get home and spend some time with Mom. You see I planned on taking a trip to see some folks I have not seen in years. It will take about 10 days, and Mom was not thrilled about that," April said.

"Now give her some slack," the Judge said. "She has been through a lot with you gone," he told her.

"Like what?" April asked.

"Well, there were some renters that made some trouble, and she had to testify in court, and YOU are her life. She worries about you. She did not know where you were or how you were doing. You know, things like that," he said.

"I know, but that is how it is. You know it. You have been where I am," April said to him.

"Well, not exactly. I was in the military, but I could write and did write to people and answered letters they wrote to me."

"I know that is difficult for her. I can't write to her and say, "Well, I was on a mission today and killed four insurgents, but rescued the one we went to retrieve," she said to him.

"Exactly, but maybe you could drop a postcard. They don't require much writing. You know like 'I was here' kind of thing. Your parents never ask for much, but a line every month or so sure would help," he said.

"Yeah, you're right," April answered him. "I get all caught up in the day-to-day things. Most are pretty intense, but a post card might relieve some of my stress as well," and she sat there contemplating. Then all at once a pillow hit her in the head, and she instinctively threw it back at a much greater speed and force.

"Hey, that was in fun. Don't try to kill me." the Judge yelled at her, and they both laughed.

"So, are you married yet?" April asked him.

The judge's face turned a bit red, and he answered, "Now you're getting a bit too nosey for your own good, but I will tell you that she and I get along very well. And we will let it at that."

In walked Missy. She looked at April and said, "He is not telling you ALL of it. They got engaged in February."

"Oh, so you're holding out on me," April said to him. "I am to tell you details on what I did, but you are evasive?"

"Oh no, it's not like that at all," the Judge said. "Yes, we got engaged, but that is no big deal. We have not made concrete plans."

April eyed him closely and said, "I forgive you, but don't do that again."

She stood up and went to hug him, but this time she felt a loss deep within her and tears began to well up in her eyes. She stepped back and told him, "I don't' know where I am going when I go back, but it has something to do with you. I get the strongest impression that is a part or about you."

The judge looked perplexed and did not know what she could mean by that. So, he said "When you find out, be sure to let me know." They hugged and she left to head home. After April left the judge pondered, he just didn't know.

She drove home and parked the car, but no one was there. She went inside and decided to make dinner for her family. As she looked around, she decided to make chicken barbeques with a large salad. She sat at the kitchen table and looked at their refrigerator. It was still the meeting place with notes on it for reminders.

April got up and went into the parlor where many of her old things were located, things like her pictures with her Olympic medals, and many scrapbooks that her Mom had made and saved for her. She found what she was looking for, Barbara Cunningham's address and Johnnie the bus driver's telephone number. She put them in her travel bag and then sat down to wait for her mom.

Within minutes Miranda came into the driveway and parked her car. She leaned into the back seat and carried two bags and something she had picked up from the dry cleaners. April went out to carry the bags for her. "Oh, thanks so much, Sweetie. I miss having you around," Miranda said. "I picked up some things for dinner, and . . ."

April interrupted her, "Mom I made dinner."

"Oh, you did? Oh, thank you, Sweetie. That was so nice of you. I know I ran late, so I really appreciate that," Miranda said.

They came in the house and April helped put the groceries away. Miranda lifted the lid of the pot that was simmering the chicken barbeque, "Mummm, that smells delicious. You are such a good daughter to me," she said.

"No, I am not. I should have written to you both. I got so wrapped up in the intense training and then going where I was asked, that I just didn't, and I am sorry," she said. "I will be more mindful when I go back," April said to her mother.

Her Mom hugged her and said, "It's all right. I am so glad you are home, even if for just a little while."

"Mom I will be back in ten days. I promise. I am going to drive out for much of the trip and fly home. I picked up a cheap cell phone in town to use while I am stateside. I am going to write down the phone number, so you have it. I will be leaving tomorrow morning though," April said.

With that the kitchen door opened and in stepped her Dad. "Hello there, Pumpkin! How are you?" he asked her.

"Good, Dad. I was just telling Mom that I am leaving tomorrow for about ten days and then you are all stuck with me for about another week. It's just that I need to see some of these

49

folks. I want to see how they are, how they are doing," she said to her Dad.

"Sounds like you have some good plans. I hope it all goes well for you," her Dad said to her.

"Well. I have not been in contact with Mrs. Cunningham from the bus trip and Johnnie the bus driver. I want to see the East too, see the Sisters in Maine, where I came from, what it is like, stop in and see Grandpa and Grandma too. I will fly home again, so I need to head out tomorrow to make it back in time.

"Will you sit down and eat dinner with us?" Dad asked her.

"Sure, I will. I wanted to help Mom, so I made it." The table was already set, so April got ice water for the three of them and sat down while Miranda doled out dinner. "No bun for me please." April said to her Mom.

"Why no bun? What are you going to eat the chicken on?" Mom asked her.

"On the plate, I just don't want bread," April answered her.

A blessing on the food was said and they all ate and had a good conversation. It was just like when she was living at home with them. Those were good times, truly, and she missed them.

That evening they had Family Home Evening. April had gathered what she needed to have a lesson. She called it "guess who". There were characters from the Bible and the Book of Mormon. Clues were written about each one, and they would have to guess who they were for points. When points were tallied there were "prizes" to choose from on a small table: gum, a small bag of potato chips, a small pin of the USA flag, and other items. It turned out to be a lot of fun. Unfortunately, they blurted out answers when it was not that person's turn, but it was all in good fun.

They said evening prayers and April went to bed early, she wanted to get a good start in the morning. She was to be at the air strip by 8 a.m. So, she kissed her parents good night and was asleep in no time.

Morning came and April woke without an alarm clock. She pressed her watch for the light to show the time, it was 5:30 a.m. She threw back her cover, made her bed, and went downstairs dressed. Dad was already up and outside feeding the ponies. April went out where he was to lend a hand. "I can do it," Gordon said. "I like these little buggers. Come over here," he said. "Remember her?"

It was Dobbins, with her big dark eyes staring at her. April called to her, "Come here, Dobbins." The pony came to her looking for a treat. She was gray on her face now. April remembered all the rides she and the pony had together. She was so dependable and safe, a big dark hairy thing with a heart of gold.

"I can't tell you how many kids have ridden on Dobbins. I lost count, but I could always count on her taking care of them," Gordon said. April knew a pony like this was one in a thousand. She always behaved and took care of inexperienced riders. "I am glad you kept her," April said.

They went in and Dad asked April, "Have you had breakfast yet?"

"No, Sir, I have not," she replied. Gordon laughed at his daughter. She did not lose the "Sir" yet. The military had instilled respect into everyone. Not that she was not respectful when she left, but since she was home every man was "Sir" and every woman "Ma'am".

51

They sat down and had breakfast, just the two of them, and then Dad put his hand on top of his daughter's. "I am so glad you came home. It means so much to your Mother and me. I know you want to travel a bit and see a few folks and I understand that. I did the very same thing. If I had not, I would never have met your Mother," and he winked at her. Soon they heard Miranda coming down the stairs. April stood up and cleared the table. She walked to her Dad and hugged him while her Mother just watched. Then she turned to her Mother and hugged her. Next she reached for her bag that was behind the living room door and stood in the kitchen ready to go.

"I wrote my cell phone number down. It is on the table in the parlor. If you need me for anything, just call. I am heading first to New Mexico to see Johnnie and then to Tennessee to see the Cunninghams. Next I will drive to the east to see where I came from and spend some time with Grandpa and Grandma. Then I will go up to Maine and see the Sisters at the convent, and to see how the school and things are going. I have not seen them since I won that race with Bitty.

After that I am calling our pilot for a ride home. I hope I am allowed to do that."

"I am sure you can," her Dad said. "You own the company."

"Okay then, I am going to head out," she kissed them both again, grabbed her bag, and was out the door.

April hopped into the old car and headed out their driveway. She headed towards the interstate for New Mexico. She enjoyed the ride. She recalled so much of what she had seen so many years ago. On route she stopped and called the number Johnnie had written down so long ago.

The phone rang three times and then she heard, "Hello."

"Hi. This is April Di Angelo. You were the bus driver that dropped me off thirteen years ago in Fresno. We went to the rodeo together and . . ."

"OH MAN! Are you kidding me. Toots, is this you?"

"Yes, it is. I was hoping to stop by. I am in New Mexico and would love to see you again," April said.

"Oh yeah, I'd love that," and he proceeded to give April directions to his house. He ended by saying, "our home is yellow and white with a flag on the front porch."

"All right then, I will be heading your way soon," she said, and in half hour she had arrived. As she drove along, she spotted his home right off the bat, it was a nice home a split level, yellow siding on the top, white on the bottom, very well kept.

April parked the car and walked up the walkway to the front door and knocked. A woman came to the door and stood there, "Hi. I am April D. I called and spoke with Johnnie. I asked if it would be okay if I stopped by for a visit," April said.

"Oh, yes. Okay, come on in," the woman said and down the steps came Johnnie.

He was older but as handsome as ever! "Toots, how are you?" he hollered. Suddenly three small boys came bounding down the stairs. "Oh boy, here is Eeny, Meeny, and Moe," Johnnie said laughing. "No, we are not," the boys hollered.

"Okay, tell the girl what your names are."

"I am. I am Dillan."

"I am Stetson."

"I am Derby," the three boys said in unison.

April smiled at them, "You all have cowboy names, fellas," and they stood there grinning at her.

"Come on in," Johnnie said to April, pulling the woman's hand up the stairs.

At the top of the steps April said, "So, Johnnie, you have three boys, Dillan, Stetson, and Derby, but the most important name you omitted," and April pointed to the woman.

"Oh, this is Koleen. She is my Irish wench," and the woman punched Johnnie in the stomach.

"I like the way you think," she said to April. "If only 'he' would think that way," Koleen said.

"We will work on that. Johnnie was always such a smooth talker, Koleen. You need to teach him that you are the most important thing in his world," April said to her.

"Now don't go giving her crazy ideas. We have it all worked out," Johnnie said.

"So, April how long are you staying? I mean two weeks or what? Koleen questioned winking to her.

"I was thinking a month. You know Johnnie is kind of hardheaded. It might take a month," and they all laughed.

"No kidding. Can you stay for a while?" Johnnie asked.

"I was planning to stay until tonight and then heading to Tennessee," April told him.

"Awe, come on. You can stay over one night and read to the boys. I know you used to love to read, and we have a lot of catching up to do. Thankfully, I don't go out until Monday, so I have a few days to give," Johnnie said.

"If Koleen says it's okay, I will stay for a bit. But I need to be back home in ten days, and I have four more stops to make," April told him.

Koleen said, "It's fine with me. I am a good judge of character and I like you," and she hugged April.

"You see, I married a schmoozer," Johnnie said laughing.

"Well, I am thrilled you settled down, and she is the best I have ever seen you with," April said to Johnnie.

After jabs and talking for a bit, they went outside into the yard. The boys wanted to play a game of softball. The youngest was on the team with Koleen and April. The two older boys, Dillan and Stetson, were on the team with Johnnie. It took some time to get used to their rules.

Old Johnnie was known to hit home runs. So, when Johnnie was up to bat, Derby pitched a low ball and "smack" Johnnie hit a line drive. April was fast getting the ball and throwing it to Koleen, who tagged Johnnie out! Johnnie was in disbelief. He called, "Unfair, unfair!" as Koleen mocked him by whining like a baby.

Then it was time for lunch. Koleen made sandwiches, the boys chomped them down, and asked for seconds. April offered to make dinner for her if she would not be offended. "Offended, I think that would be awesome," Koleen said.

So, for dinner April made a quick stop at the grocery store. She had the boys go with her to show her the way. She bought chicken, ravioli, garlic bread, and some things that the boys asked for.

Back at Johnnie's, they unloaded their bags and April started to make fried chicken, ravioli, and garlic bread.

Dinner was at 5:00 p.m. sharp the boys helped April set the table and then she told them to go and get their Mom and Dad. Stetson called to them from the hallway, "Oh, love birds, dinner is ready."

April was amused and grateful that Johnnie found someone to love who loved him right back. They were a good match and three boys, how awesome. Now Johnnie had a good reason to come home.

Soon they were all sitting down at the table and Johnnie tapped Dillan's hand that had been reaching for chicken. "What?" Dillan asked.

"Just wait," his Dad said to him. "April, will you say grace?" Johnnie wanted to know.

"Sure, thanks," April said. She offered grace and the boys stared at her trying to comprehend.

After grace was said, Stetson asked, "Where did you learn that?"

"I go to church," April answered him. "Ask your Mom or Dad to take you so you can learn to do it too," and she winked at him.

Koleen said, "I wanted to take them to church, but he won't go with us."

"I never have time," Johnnie said in his defense.

"If you don't make the time, they will not stop growing and wait for you. Time keeps marching on," April told him.

"Yeah, you're right. Ahhhh, there is never enough time," Johnnie said frustrated.

"You need to time management. Again, if you went to church you could be taught that too," April told him. "Prioritize, prioritize, prioritize!"

"Why don't you take the kids and go by yourself, Koleen?" April asked her.

"I think I will," Koleen said. "That way when he is home, he won't have any excuse like he usually has. 'I don't know where to go. I don't know anyone there.' Yep, I think you got this right, April. My boys need direction, and they have questions I can't answer," Koleen said.

That night April read books to the boys. They were all huddled around her, begging as each book ended, "One more, just one more."

Johnnie said to April "You're going to make a great Momma someday, Toots. Just look at you with my boys, like a mother hen with her chicks," and he laughed.

Soon it was bedtime and they boys grumbled a bit as they rubbed their tired eyes. April knelt beside one of their beds, she encouraged them to do the same, and they did. She said a prayer for them and about them. When she finished Dillon said, "Mom, we want to go to church to learn how to pray like she does."

"Okay," Koleen said. "Next week don't whine to me that you are sleepy and don't want to get up. We are all going."

Before April retired, she had a candid talk with Johnnie and Koleen about what her life had been like since he dropped her off in Fresno 16 years ago. Johnnie said, "I was going to take you with me, but something nagged at me not to. I was so torn to let you in a place where no one came to claim you. It sickened me. You were the cutest, smartest kid ever and I would have been happy to raise you with Fred."

When Koleen said, "Oh, I can see how well that would have turned out. You might be working by dancing in a lounge or pole dancing."

April said, "It all worked out for the best for all of us, of that I have no doubt." She then told them about the church and how it had changed her life, even in the military. She said, "I feel as if I was meant to be here." After a while April told them she was tired. She was shown a place to sleep in their basement where Koleen had made up a bed for her on a couch in their den. April said a prayer but later did not remember it. She was that tired.

April was up first and made breakfast. Johnnie was up next. "I remember this scene," he laughed.

"Well, I am a bit older now, and a much better cook." With that Koleen came into the kitchen as someone was knocking on their door. It was Johnnie's sister, her husband, and their three boys.

"Come on in," Koleen said to them, and in bound the three rambunctious boys looking for their cousins.

"How are you!" exclaimed red haired Wendy and her husband Tom. "Gosh, we have thought about you so many times and asked Johnnie about you, but he said he lost touch with you."

April explained briefly what she had already told Johnnie. They all sat down to a nice breakfast but had to put a smaller card table up to seat all the boys. The four oldest would sit at the small card table and the youngest two from each family sat at the big table with the adults.

"How long are you staying?" Tom asked April.

"I really should be leaving today. I have four more stops, and with the traffic. I just need to keep moving," she answered them.

"We are so glad Johnnie called us to come to see you again. If you are ever here in New Mexico, stop in and see us.

"Well, I will be going back to active duty the middle of October. I only had twenty days leave. I will see how it goes," she said to her.

"Don't worry about cleaning up. You do what you need to do to get going," Johnnie said to her.

When they were finished eating, April stood up to leave the table, gather her things, and repack. Thankfully Koleen did wash the few things she did have soiled, they were folded and setting on the den's steps. Bag in hand she climbed the steps. They were in living room, some of the boys were there playing with matchbox cars.

Johnnie stood up and said, "Are you ready to ship out, Toots?" April laughed at him.

"Will I ever lose that name and be me?"

"Probably not," he answered her. They hugged a long hug of rekindled friendship, and then Koleen was next, followed by Tom and Wendy. Johnnie handed April an envelope, "Here this is for you. All of us contributed and wanted to help you on your journey."

April was taken aback. She did not need the money, but she knew she had to take it, or they would be offended. She humbly thanked them and headed out. Someday she would repay them. She just had to.

April backed out of the driveway onto the street, beeped good-bye, and headed out toward Tennessee. She knew she should fill up on gas. So, the first gas station she found with a decent price, she stopped. April went in to pay and bought a cold bottle of water and two trail mix bars in case she got hungry before she got to her next destination. She hopped in, buckled up her seatbelt, and headed to the state highway. She turned on the radio looking for a station she liked. She searched for smooth country music. She loved Hank Williams and the old stuff. If not she could pop in a CD, there were several in the glove box. This was going to be a long ride. "Tennessee, here I come," she said to herself.

For the drive to Tennessee, she decided to stay with the flow of traffic, but also take her time. The first full day of driving, April decided to rent a motel room and get a decent meal. There was no sense putting herself at risk. She chose a reputable motel line that served food. She checked in and prepaid for the night. Then she took her bag with to her room. She swiped the card in the door and remembered Barbara.

In her room she rang the lobby and asked if there was a way to look up telephone numbers. The woman on the other end said they had telephone books down in the lobby, but they also had Wi-Fi so she could look on the computer.

April put on a dress that was cool and comfortable and her sandals and headed downstairs. She went to the lobby and asked where the Wi-Fi was. The woman pointed to an area where there were one or two people sitting on computers. She sat down at one of the computers and logged on. She typed in the Cunningham's address and searched for their telephone number, nothing. So, she downloaded the driving directions, printed the sheet and paid fifty cents for them.

April headed to the restaurant. Just inside the door was a young woman who waited to seat her. "Do you prefer a table or a booth?" she asked April.

"A table please," April said and soon she was sitting midway in the restaurant looking at her menu. She chose the stuffed chicken breast and a salad. The description sounded delicious, so she thought she would try it.

April sat there and looked around waiting for her food to arrive. It was nice to be able to get a meal and this was a nice place. But she loved eating at home more than dining out. This place was almost empty. She remembered eating with Barbara and smiled to herself. She hoped to see her soon. Her food came and it was better than she hoped. They served garlic bread with her meal. She barely finished and had no room for dessert.

April headed to her room and undressed. She opted for a nice warm shower to wash off the dust and sweat from the long drive. She donned on a white nightgown, pulled down the covers and laid in the bed. It was almost 10 p.m., and she knew she would want to get up by 3, so she had better sleep.

At 3:15 a.m. April awoke as usual without an alarm clock. She listened to the sounds to acclimate herself to where she was. Then she got up, dressed, and packed to go again. She stopped at the restaurant, but it was closed. But there was a complimentary snack bar, so she took some apples, fruit bars, and an 8-ounce container of 2% milk with her.

April got into her car and soon was on the road again. She had about four hundred more miles to go and was determined to make it by the end of the day. On the road there were many truckers who were carrying America on their loads. April remembered how she and her Dad would go to the auctions and haul ponies home. She would always fall asleep as her Daddy drove. When she was older, she did the driving and never was tired. Her Dad used to tease her about that.

By noon April felt confident she would be at Barbara's by late afternoon. She stopped for gasoline when the tank was near a third full and took a break every 6 hours. It was a rather nice drive. The traffic was minimal, no one was making any problems, and every vehicle kept moving.

By 5:00 p.m. April was turning into what felt like a familiar street and then she saw the Cunningham's home. It was the only one like it with its huge overhangs and big yard. April parked out front and went to the front door and ring the doorbell.

A woman came to the door and asked her, "May I help you?"

April explained she was looking for Barbara and Kyle Cunningham who had lived here thirteen years ago. The woman did not recall that name and apologized to April. April stood there for a minute to decide what to do next. If they moved, surely they would be in the telephone directory. But it was now after 5:00 p.m. and no one would answer the telephone. So, she did the next best thing. As she drove, she spotted a state police officer. She slowed down, stopped, and got out of her car to ask for his help. The officer looked at her suspiciously at first, and April handed him her license. Within five minutes the officer was more than helpful.

"I didn't recognize you," he said.

"Oh?" April asked him.

"I am Bob's son. I sort of remember you from that day at the lake. Do you remember?" he asked her. "If you follow me, I can take you to where my grandparents live," he said to April.

What luck, the first officer she asked, and he is related to the Cunningham's. April touched his arm and asked him, "Why did your grandparent's move?"

"Well, Grandpop had a heart attack about eight years ago, and then the following year he had two more right in a row. Grandma could not keep up the house, the yard, and stuff, so she decided to put the house up for sale. They moved into a smaller ranch home to be close to town and near stores and such. She is very active, but Grandpop, not so much. She takes him along with her almost all the time though," he told April.

April felt bad. How ignorant it was of her to assume that this family would be here just as she left it. Time marches on, bringing changes, both good and bad.

Health is so important and to try to stay healthy, she just felt bad. As she followed the officer, she realized that she had forgotten to ask his name. She never had been to this area of their town. It reminded her of home. It had big trees all around the area, the homes were all in good shape, and everyone waved to the officer. They probably had seen him visiting with his grandparents before. They stopped on the street and the officer waited for April. Together they walked to the front porch.

On his shirt tag it said "Cunningham", and April asked him, "What is your first name?"

"Troy," he said as the door opened, and there stood Barbara.

Troy said to her, "I found this person snooping around your house and I wanted to ask if you want to press charges?" Barbara's face showed alarm and slowly it changed as she looked at April. Then suddenly, she burst into tears as she stepped forward to hug the little girl she loved and had let go so long ago. The two of them hugged and cried tears of joy at their reunion.

"Oh, look at me. Come in. Come in," Barbara said. "Kyle, Kyle come out here and see who came to see us." never taking her eyes off April. Hal came out using a walker, it was evident Hal had suffered a stroke as well. His face was slanted to the side, his speech was slurred, and he was difficult to understand.

April was choked up. It was Troy who saved the moment. "Well, I must go. I have my checkpoints to do, and I am just glad she found me before she did any other officer. That request sounded funny. It's almost a miracle you did find me," he said.

The three of them sat in the living room and Barbara went on to explain about why they moved and what had happened to Kyle. Although the change was a little hard on them, it was easier living here. The house was all on one floor, shopping was close by, and all the neighbors were so nice. April was happy for them.

Then the questions came to April. What had she been doing, and so on. Barbara brought out the letters April and her Mom had written to her twelve years earlier. She had saved them all this time and was deeply touched. April could easily see now why she had to move on to the unknown all those years ago. She would have been a burden for the Cunninghams making life harder on them. Yes, sir. God sure knew what he was doing then and now.

They talked about what April did since her arrival in California just briefly an overview. April did tell Barbara she reconnected with her birth Mother and how that happened and about her grandfather. Barbara was genuinely happy for her. "How long can you stay?" Barbara asked her.

"I thought I'd visit a bit and go. I am heading to Maine," she told her.

"Can you stay overnight and have dinner with us?" Barbara begged. April knew their circumstances had changed drastically so as tactfully and as kindly as she could muster, she wanted to explain to her.

"Maine is such a long way off yet, and I have to be back home in a few days. But my heart is with you. You know that. I have spent many hours thinking about you both, hoping I would see you again, and now I have. I am so grateful for your love and care for me so long ago. I can only imagine what a burden I was," April said to Barbara.

"Oh, no, you were not. You were a delight to have. And I would have kept you, but now I do see that it was all for the best that you went home."

April got up to hug and kiss Barbara. She became suddenly emotional. "I love you, Barbara. You mean so much to me. My words fall far short of what I am feeling. I will stay in touch with you, I promise. I will never forget you or your kindness."

April took Barbara's address with her and said her goodbyes, then walked out to her car, and headed back out to the highway. She did not see officer Troy, perhaps his shift was over. But she offered a silent prayer of thanks to a very kind Father in Heaven who again helped her find who she needed on her journey.

Tennessee to Pennsylvania was going to be a long haul, so April decided to make the best of it and enjoy the trip. When she fueled up, she got some rest. When she got up on Rt. 80, she drove through a town called DuBois. It was a medium-sized town and she decided to get some lunch. She chose a small Italian restaurant right downtown. Its name was Tommy D's. It was midday, the traffic was minimal, and parking was easy. April saw a curious listing on the menu, chicken salad. It was cut up chicken (or beef) on a bed of salad, along with hand cut French fries, topped with cheese and your preferred dressing. That salad was outstanding, and she was bowled over by the hand-squeezed lemonade. It was a very good supper.

April liked this small quaint town. The people were so friendly, but she could not stay. She had to keep going. She had to be cautious and watch for the Northeast Extension. The Rt. 80 highway was nice, two lanes on the left and two lanes on the right, with big trees and grass in the middle. The scenery was beautiful.

When she got near the exit she wanted, she saw a restaurant, and decided to have some lunch. It was a very nice place, clean, and cheery inside. The waitresses were very friendly, and she opted for tomato soup and a grilled cheese sandwich. It was good, but not like her Mom's. But all in all, a good experience. If she was ever through this way again, she would gladly stop.

On she went. In forty-five minutes, she was getting off the interstate, paid her tolls, and was headed toward the town where her grandparents lived. She noticed that the towns were mainly German Catholic, with temple towers on tops of the churches. The craftsmanship was outstanding and very impressive.

April had the address and looked for the street. She got twisted around a bit, so she asked for directions, and was kindly given the exact directions by a stranger. The house was on the outskirts of town along a little-used road. April pulled alongside the road and sat there for a minute.

April noticed someone came outside and began to water flowers and what was left of their garden. It was obviously a woman because she had a dress on, but it did not look like her grandmother.

April got the little amount of possessions she wanted to take into their home and got out of the car. She walked up to the side door on the porch and rang the doorbell. The door opened and there was her grandmother, she smiled, and welcomed April in. Her Grandmother said Grandpop was at the store and would be home soon.

"Sit down. Are you hungry or want something to drink?" she asked April.

"Oh, no. Thank you. I am fine," April replied. "You have a lovely home," she remarked.

"Oh, it's nothing much. When we retired from farming, we felt we should have a smaller home with everything on one floor. But this home does have a basement and a big yard," as her Grandmother motioned with her arm to the window.

"Yes, I saw that. It is a lot of weeding," April exclaimed.

"He likes to garden. He keeps the garden going and tends a small flock of chickens in the back pen," and she walked away to put water in a kettle to set it on the stove for tea.

"I like my tea. Sometimes my stomach is not so good," the old woman said. April wondered if she had seen a doctor about her condition, and then the woman handed April a prescription bottle, "Here is what I am taking for my stomach, but I don't like taking it so much," she said.

"Well, I was told by my doctor that I should stay on a medicine until the bottle was empty. The medicine needs time to work in the body and sometimes it may take a while," April told her.

"Ah, it's nothing really. Nothing my tea does not help me with," and she winked at April. April realized this woman was a determined woman, not stubborn, but wanted to do things her own way. Maybe she got some of her genes after all, and April smiled.

They sat at the table for a while talking about what was in the town, about family members who she knew, and what they were doing when the door opened, and in walked Grandpop. "Oh, my April," he exclaimed excitedly. "You have come to visit us," as he dropped the bags onto the floor to embrace her.

"Let me help you with those," April said to him.

"No, no. Those can wait," he said, and he and his wife looked at each other. In his own language he asked his wife how long the girl was here, "Only a few minutes," she told him. "Come, come and sit in on the couch and be comfortable," he asked of April.

As they sat in the living room, which was quite small and quaint, they began a whale of a conversation. As family members names were mentioned that were not familiar to April, Grandpop had a revelation, a big idea. "We have a party, right here. They come. They meet you, and you know," he said with a big smile on his face.

Grandma was not so thrilled. "Why do you want a party here?" she asked.

"So they know where to come," he answered her quickly.

April protested lightly, "You do not need to throw a party or go out of your way. I am so grateful to be here and visit with you. I have some time, but not a lot, for you see I have not been back to Maine to see how everyone is since the race."

"Oh, yes. I remember that," Grandpop said. "We can have party here," he kept saying. April kept looking at Grandma who clearly did not want a party HERE! So, when Grandma got up to go into the kitchen, April followed her with her cup for a refill.

"Please, you do not need to have a party here. Is there a church that will allow a meeting in their basement or a community center?" April asked. Her Grandma's eyes opened wide, "Yes, the church. The church will allow a family gathering for a little money. April went to the small kitchen table and took out her cell phone. She dialed Mr. Stevens and spoke with him. April paused for a moment looking at her grandmother and said, "What is the address here again, please?"

Her grandmother said it and April repeated it to Mr. Stevens. "Thank you so much, really," April said to the man, and hung up. There will be a next day delivery of a check, so you take it and plan the party he wants. I never wanted to make a burden on you."

"Oh, no. He will not want that. He will be angry, upset," her grandmother said to her looking alarmed.

"Well, what he does not know will not hurt him," April said smiling to her grandmother. The old woman bent over a bit and began to chuckle.

Back in the living room, to make it appear as if it were her idea, grandmother told Grandpop she would call the church to rent the basement with the kitchen. There would be too many people that will come into the home and their home was too small. On that Grandpop had to agree.

And so that is how a party in the beginning of October happened in that tiny, quaint little town. The church was very accommodating and kind. There was so much food it could have fed an army. Grandpop was in his glory, taking April from person to person and explaining who they were. April did not grasp all their names. It was impossible. There were over a hundred people there, coming and going. From person to person, some standing, some sitting at a table eating, some were sitting on chairs along the wall. It seemed endless, but April knew that her grandparents were proud of her, and they wanted all their family to know who she was, and she was theirs.

Then Grandpop took April to two men who were sitting at the far end of the basement. They had plates balanced on their laps holding their drinks. When he approached them, both men set their food dishes and drinks down and stood up to greet them.

"These are your brothers, Tim and John," Grandpop said. This was indeed an emotional moment for April. She stepped forward to hug them and the three of them had tears in their eyes. They could not let go for quite some time. April pulled up a chair to talk with them.

They told her it was the two of them who put her on that bus so very long ago. No one knew it was them until recently when their Mother left for California. They said their Dad didn't care. "He is over there now. He is the one with the glasses and partially bald. Can you see him?" John asked her. April looked and saw a sad sight. It was almost pitiful. He was a thin man about 5' 9" tall, small framed, with glasses and balding. The man never looked in their direction or seemed to take notice of what the party was about. Her father certainly did not look anything like her Father or Mother.

"Were you two all right? I mean I don't remember much about back then, but I know I was afraid of him," April said.

"Yeah, when we were little kids, we were all afraid of him," Tim mused. "But when we got older, we could run away, then drive away. He never got to us," Tim said.

"And if he tried, it was two against one," John added.

"This was awful, so very sad," thought April. If only they had the Father she had, one who wanted his children with him. She said nothing, but she did not care if she met her biological Father or not.

Grandpop had other ideas. He took April by her hand, looked at the boys and told them she would be back, and led her to her Father. Grandpop stood there for a while and felt like he was being ignored. He made a noise with his throat as if he was clearing it, "Ahem". Then his son looked at him and then quickly looked away again.

"I thought you would like to meet your daughter. It is about time you recognize her for the wonderful person she has become away from your influence."

That was not expected, and it made April feel very uncomfortable. She looked at her feet. She did not want to look at him. He had treated her ignorantly, cruelly, and very mean. No one would ever do that to her again, not ever. She felt she did not need this in her life and tugged at Grandpop to walk away. Grandpop stood his ground and held onto April's hand.

Her Father was having a good time talking with some women. They all had drinks in their hands and April wondered how they got alcohol into the church. Then she noticed a bottle hanging out of one woman's purse. Wonderful she thought, breaking rules, and no thought of what others would suffer because of their actions. April was beginning to feel embarrassed, upset, and angry.

She loosened her hand from her grandfather's and walked straight to the woman with the purse on her shoulder. She pulled the bottles of whiskey and vodka from the purse and handed the bottles to her grandfather across the table. "Hey, you can't do that," the woman shouted at April.

"I can and I did," April said to her. "Rules are for everyone, including YOU." With that April began to walk away when she felt someone or something pulling at the back of her shirt.

She half turned and saw her Father pulling at her saying some not so nice things. With one swipe of her hand April loosened his grip on her shirt and faced him. "Is there something you want to say to me, Sir?" April said to him while straightening her shirt and standing tall.

"You think you are smart. Don't you? You have an attitude. I could have changed if your darn Mother had kept out of it, but no, you were her princess," he said.

April cut him off. "Listen, you have little to say to me about how to raise a child. You failed big time, many times. My Father is a good man, and you fall short of being a good man. You are more interested in what you want. You don't lift her finger to help anyone," she told him.

The man was taken aback. No one spoke to him like this. He raised his hand to strike her when April said, "Go ahead. I dare you to hit me. You will find yourself lying on the floor with a broken arm. I guarantee that!" April turned from him and strode across the floor with her grandfather following her. Grandpop was smiling from ear to ear.

She sat down again with her two brothers and Grandpop standing there chuckling to himself. "You told him April," he said.

The two brothers were watching their father and said, "Man is he pissed. Look at that. Just look at him."

April refused, she would not. "I don't get any enjoyment out of seeing someone acting ignorant or mean. He is nothing more than a spoiled child, acting out a temper tantrum. I rightfully put him in his place, and he did not like it. That's too bad for him. Others should have done this all his life and he would not be the sourly cur he is now," she said. "I swear if he ever lays a hand on me, I will break his bones. I know how and I will do it."

The party went on through the evening without any incident. Her biological Father left shortly after they had exchanged words. He left with the two women. The brothers were her escorts throughout the party. They knew everyone and had a lot to say about her.

Her brothers asked her many, many questions about her past life and her future plans. They both joked a lot too. One would say something, and the other would add to it, then they would laugh. April kind of remembered them being like this. Somehow it was still there, but not fully.

The party ended late. April had a pocket full of addresses with telephone numbers and most importantly the addresses of her two brothers who did not live with their Dad. She helped to clear tables, sort dishes, glasses, and silverware and then she washed them in the kitchen.

There were several who stayed behind to help including her brothers who seemed like they wanted to ask her something. And finally, John did, "So are there any good jobs out there near you?" They both stood there waiting for a reply.

"Well, there are, but it depends on your experience and qualifications," she said. "What can you do?" she asked them. They looked at each other, shrugging, and began to laugh. "Can you drive trucks, tandems, tractors, tractor trailer rigs? What is the class of your license? You know things like that," she said. They began to think and verbally say many things. The more they spoke the better they felt, and they laughed at each other many times. April watched them from time to time and thought there would never be a dull moment with these two.

By 11:30 p.m. they were leaving the church basement. Grandmother said, "I am thankful we had this party on a Friday evening instead of a Saturday. I would be too tired in the morning to get up for church."

April agreed with her one hundred percent. She was overly tired because of the travel and the emotions, and this was a very late evening even for her.

April slept on a small twin bed they had for visitors in a small bedroom. It was good enough to sleep and there was a small dresser she could put her small suitcase on. Sleep came fast, but she was up very early as her body took over.

At 3:00 a.m. she was sitting in the living room reading an old newspaper waiting for them to get up. Grandpop came out about 5:00 a.m. and told her, "get dressed up," they were going out for breakfast. Within ten minutes she and her grandfather were walking to the garage to get Grandpop's car to go into town for breakfast.

They headed to a small restaurant in town, parked, and went in. Everyone knew each other and said "hello" or waved as they entered. They passed by booths to the next open spot where they sat down. A waitress brought over a menu and asked how they were. Grandpop just nodded his head. He and April looked over their menus.

"This one is good," Grandpop pointed to a picture of eggs with sausage or bacon with toast.

"It looks like a lot to eat to me," April winked at him.

Grandpop smiled and said, "Oh, my April, you are something." She ordered one Belgian waffle with strawberries and a large milk to drink. Grandpop ordered his favorite meal that came out on three dishes. The two of them were often interrupted with conversations from all around them. April thought it was interesting that they had conversations this way, just shout out to a friend, and they answered you. It was not private, but news for everyone there.

When they were finished, April snapped up the check before the waitress had a chance to lay it on the table. "No" Grandpop said, as he reached for the bill.

April told him, "Absolutely. I pay, and you let the tip."

"Okay, my April," Grandpop said. He was very impressed with her. She was so young and strong, in mind and body. And she was kind and had high standards. They left and he took her for a little ride.

"Where are we going, Grandpop?" she asked him.

"You see," he answered her. They drove for a while through town, up a side street, this way and that, making turns, and soon there was a cemetery in sight. Grandpop slowed the car down and turned onto the cemetery property. "Come, we get out. I show you," he said to his granddaughter.

He stood there pointing, "Do you see over there, the little area with metal bars? There lay asleep two of our children."

April was shocked, how awful. She took her Grandpop by his hand and the two of them walked over to the small grave. "I come every weekend to see them," he told her.

April was speechless. Their names were Rosa and Jime. "What happened?" April asked him softly.

"Rosa was still born. All there, beautiful little girl, but not breathing. And Jime was hit by a car as he was walking along side of the road. He was only seven years old." With that Grandpop took out his hanky, wiped his eyes, and blew his nose.

"I am so sorry," April said. "I wish I had known them." Grandpop reached over and hugged her.

"You know for a long time I thought you were gone, like them," he said with his hand quickly motioning in the direction of the graves, with tears rolling down his face.

"Oh, Grandpop, I am so sorry. I know it must have been difficult for you, but you see now that it was the best thing. You see that. Don't you?" she asked him.

"Yes, of course I see it. But, April, we lost so much time, knowing each other, doing things together, and so much more," he said.

She reached over and hugged him again, and he hugged her right back. "I love you, Grandpop, more than my words can ever say. I never want to lose you. I need you in my life. You are such a good, good man. I am honored to have you as my grandfather. The two of them stood there for a while on that chilly Saturday morning in November as the sun began to break up the clouds.

"Come we go now, or she will wonder where we are," with his hands he made his fingers go up and down as if a mouth was arguing. April said nothing, she imagined that the two of them got into spats, but she also believed he walked away. In the time he spent with them in California he showed only steady serene patience.

They got into his car and drove slowly home, the long way around. When they arrived, he parked in the garage, they got out, and Grandma was there in the breezeway waiting for them. "Have you had breakfast?" she asked them. He just nodded his head and walked into the house.

April met up with her and said, "We went to the graveside."

"He always goes," Grandma said, and they went inside.

Grandpa sat down with the newspaper and buried his nose. April was unsure what to do. She went into the kitchen where her grandmother was peeling potatoes. "I make supper," she said.

"I can help you," April replied to her. So, she picked up some carrots and began to clean them. Then she cut the onion in slices.

"You cook much?" her grandmother asked.

"Not a lot, but I like to cook," April said to her.

"That's good. Learn to cook and make different recipes, so you are not bored in the kitchen. I like spices. Here smell this," and she handed April a bottle of saffron and then some marjoram.

"I like the second one best," April said to her.

"Yes, it is light and airy, and very good in a roast no matter if it is beef or pork or chicken, it is always better" Grandmother said.

April looked at the time. It was already past noon. "Grandma, I don't think I will be here for supper. I should be heading out for Maine soon. I really hoped to be there for mass on Sunday morning."

"Auk, you stay. You young and can drive all night. No?"

Grandpop heard this and came into the kitchen. "April, you no go so soon. Stay for supper and leave very early to get to mass," he said.

"Grandpop, I am looking at a five-hour drive, so I need time to get there and be ready," April said to him.

"Okay. How about you eat and then go," and his hands went over one another in a go motion. April sighed silently. She would do it somehow but was not sure how. She knew she would get sleepy driving with a full tummy. She had some good CDs and could sing along. That would keep her awake.

She sat quietly in the living room as the meal was in the oven, she closed her eyes and concentrated on the sounds and smells in this house. She loved older people's homes. They had character, a lived-in feeling, and smells. April could smell the smell of her grandmother's perfume on the chair she was sitting on.

Her grandfather's cologne was on the pillow on her lap. Her legs were stretched out with her feet on an ottoman, and she listened. She could hear the furnace chugging to keep the house warm, and she could hear when the water was turned on. The pipes made a screeching noise, and the water made a low bang when turned off. She could hear crows outside calling, and the occasional scratch on the window in the kitchen from a small tree that had grown too close to the house and its branches scraped at the window. April was almost asleep when she heard a car door bang with someone yelling. She opened her eyes and realized she was alone.

She got up and looked out the kitchen window. There they were. Her grandparents in the backyard. Grandpop was tending his chickens, and grandmother was tending some kale in the garden. It was a gray day. The sun disappeared behind clouds, and the wind began to kick up a bit. It was definitely cooler here in October. She put on her jacket to go out and be part of what they were doing.

Her grandmother asked her to hold a bag while she cut off the Kale and then she pulled some winter onions and the last cabbage in the garden. "I make halupki tomorrow. You like halupki?"

April did. They were cabbage leaves that were separated, boiled lightly, removed from the water to cool. Then cooked hamburger and rice is put into the center of the cabbage leaf, folded and rolled, and secured with a toothpick. They get baked in a Dutch oven with sauce.

"No, I love them," she laughingly said to her grandmother.

"You silly girl," her grandmother replied. "Go check on him," she said to April.

Grandpop was with his chickens who were obviously pets, "Come, chick, chick, come and eat," he called to them.

The hens came out of their coop and walked around pecking at cracked corn kernels. Grandpop asked April to go to the back of the coop and open the small door that showed the back of the nesting boxes. Sure enough, there were six eggs there. April put the eggs into a small plastic bucket that was hanging on the coop on a nail.

"Here you go Grandpop" she said.

Grandpop took the egg bucket and said, "You come in here." What he meant was to come into the garage. It was not heated, but it was out of the wind. He pulled up two chairs, sat down on one, and April sat on the other.

"So, my April, I must tell you that I was to the doctor, and he says I am sick. He says I must have blood drawn and tests. So, I tell you this in case things don't go so good," her Grandpop said to her.

April was stunned. "No!" she screamed inside.

"Oh, my April, don't look so unhappy. We all die, you know? I am 79 now."

April looked directly into her Grandpop's eyes. "Grandpop, I am going to ask you to do something for me, please! Will you allow me to have someone give you a blessing? For comfort and for healing if it is God's will."

He looked directly at her, and said, "I say okay."

April knew as honest as he was being with her, he was not telling her everything. She felt that he would never have brought this up if this sickness was not somewhat serious. "Grandpop, I am going to Maine tonight and leaving in two days to come back. I need to know how you are. I am asking you, nope I am begging you, to let me, let us, help you," she said to him.

"April, you no come back right away. My test not until Thursday. You stay a few days and then come back after my test," Grandpop said to her.

April asked, "How about I come here on Thursday to go along with you to the test?"

Grandpop was pleased. He did not want to burden anyone with this, but he was so impressed at her willingness. She had been taught well. Family was important, and he was happy she loved him because the love he had for her went deep, to his very soul.

They got up from their chairs and went outside. As they walked to the house, they turned to see who was behind them coming through the gate. It was the two brothers, Tim and John. They all headed inside for a delicious warm, rib-sticking meal.

The boys were curious about jobs, since there were few in the area. April wrote down Mr. Steven's telephone number for them to call and speak to him directly. "Jobs are not all in California. They are in almost every state. You call him, he will advise you, and set you up for an interview," she told them.

"An interview! Don't you own these farms?" one brother asked her.

"I do and I don't. It is a corporation. I do not oversee the jobs or know the criteria for them. This company is so big it spans across America. The jobs are endless – from butcher, truck driver, mechanics, barn managers, regular workers on the farms, and custom farming. I cannot say all the jobs there are, but he will know. Talk with him. He is a really nice man.

Grandmother agreed, "He was kind to us. Showed us all around. He is smart man. You say prayers for us" and she tapped April's hand.

So, after many conversations at the table, April kept a keen eye on her Grandpop who seemed to have trouble eating. He burped a lot and drank a lot of water. April looked at the clock it was now 7 p.m. She half suspected he had a hernia or irritation in the stomach or lining. But since she was not a doctor, it would be best to have tests to rule things out one by one to get to the root of the problem. But Thursday would hopefully reveal what to do next. She asked to be excused from the table, and the boys joked at that. She gathered up her things, adjusted her jacket, and went to the door. Everyone stood and hugged her.

Grandmother handed her something wrapped in a real cloth hankie. "I will be back in a few days," she said.

"Oh," said Grandmother. "Maybe you can drive us. I don't like city driving." April assured them she would arrive to take them to their appointment which was at 1:00 p.m. on Thursday. She reached for her small bag, Tim held the door for her, and she walked out to her car. They followed her to the curb and watched her. She waved but was not sure if they saw her. It was already nightfall. The days were much shorter, and it was dark by 5:30 p.m. She started the car's engine and pulled out. She headed into town to fill the gas tank and was on the turnpike in fifteen minutes.

The ride to Maine was good. There were very few cars out on the road, mostly truckers who were great drivers. April never drove in packs anyway, so she turned on her radio and sang along to the songs. She liked most all music, country was her favorite, but she also liked pop music, everyday stuff, some musicals from movies, and the oldies. She was not a fan of rap or soul mainly because she did not understand it. She grew up in the country, not the city. At her first stop for gas, she picked up a flashlight since she did not have one in the car.

April made exceptionally good time. She did speed a bit, but just to keep up with the flow of traffic. She arrived at her destination by 10:30 that evening. She knew of a small hotel, checked in, and flopped on the bed. She was almost asleep in her clothing, but the bathroom yellow light bothered her, and she got up to turn it off. She undressed and took a shower in the dark. She made very little noise. She did not turn the television on. She pulled out her small scriptures and began to read a bit. She needed comfort from the news about her Grandpop. When she felt ready, she got on her knees by the bedside and began to pray. She prayed for her Grandpop that the tests would not be severe, for her grandmother to accept what was to be, and for her parents back home. She asked a blessing for tomorrow, that all would go well she did not want special attention, just to see how they were. She prayed about other things and then began to feel tired.

April pulled back the sheets and crawled into bed. The room was very dark, and it was quiet. Sleep greeted her quickly allowing her to arise by 4 a.m. She was up, packed, and ready to go but knew no one was at the church yet. So out came her scriptures again. At 6:00 a.m. she walked to the office, turned in her key, paid the bill, and got into her car. She thought about a small diner that was not far away, so she headed there.

It was an old railroad car, shiny silver, very quaint, and the food was all homemade. She ordered an egg over easy on a half slice of bread, grits, and a cup of hot cocoa with marshmallows. She felt stuffed, paid her bill, and left for church. She was sitting in a pew by 7:10 a.m., ample time for the 8:00 mass.

April did not recognize the older Priest that was officiating, but she did see some of the Sisters from the past sitting in the pews up in the balcony. She was in full uniform out of respect for her unit, country, and God, and felt no one would recognize her. When mass was over, a young altar boy came to her, handing her a note. She stood there and opened the note. It read: "I think I know you, so if this is indeed you, our girl who helped us not so long ago, please join us after mass at home."

April looked around but saw no one. She knew where to go. She exited the church by a side door and walked the thirty yards to the big complex she had gifted them. She stood at the door and knocked. A novice opened the door, and as she did seven sisters came rushing the door all talking at once, pulling her inside. April was laughing so hard. She could not contain herself. The nuns were so happy to see her. Then they heard the harsh hand clapping, "Sisters, Sisters, what is the meaning of this noise and outbursts?" It was Mother Superior at last. She stood there with a pursed smile on her lips and said, "I should have known it was you. You always did make disruptions" and she stepped forward to embrace April while the nuns stood around them sighing.

"You know I have two other masses to attend, and I must be there," Mother Superior said to April.

"I know and I will be there too," April replied to her. So, they walked down the hall for a bite to eat and a little something to rinse it down. They again walked the halls to the church. April sat in a pew in the back. It was nice to see the church fill up at this 10:00 service with families including children of all ages. April could not help but smile at mothers' frustration to keep their small children quiet. The children were so innocent. "I guess all moms go through this," she thought.

The music from the organ played, the choir sang, and the incense was pungent in the air. April began to feel sleepy. The church was a haven for her - not so long ago when life was confusing, and she needed answers. Yes, it had been good to her, when there was no family around her, they became her family. How could she not love the church, it was almost impossible to serve someone with all she had and then not love them.

The organ payed a solemn song as the congregation sang and began to file outside. April stood up, put her cap in her hand, and began to exit the church through the side door once more. There she met several nuns that she had known previously. They were all smiles wanting to talk to her. They walked along at a fast pace. The nuns had a schedule to keep. First would be lunch, then they wanted to show April the grounds, and what they had done with them. It was a lot to take in. April wanted to wait for Mother Superior, but the Sisters assured April that she was busy and wanted April to go along with them to see the grounds.

At the school the rooms smelled like any school, the smell of pencils, crayons, and books. It was wonderful. Those smells sent April back to her elementary school days, eating that thick white paste that tasted so good. A lump on a piece of paper used sparingly to glue your project and eat the rest. April almost laughed out loud.

It was obvious there were many children using the school, as there were thirty-two names on the coatrack. The Sunday school was in full swing after church and the rooms swelled with noisy children.

April was so grateful. Way back then she could not see all the good from this, but she did know the Sisters would do all they could to serve God.

Next on to the big kitchen. The smells coming from that room were a dead giveaway. April could smell apples, like apple pie baking. "There are apple pancakes this morning for the children who have no lunch at home. A slice of ham, pancakes, and milk. And each will take an apple home with them," one nun said. That was wonderful, a child does not know poor, but they can feel poor mainly in their tummies. That was unfair to them because they cannot change their home situation. The smallest good can make a huge difference to a child. April was more than pleased. What a wonderful job these nuns were doing under the guidance of Mother Superior.

Then everyone went into the huge room in the middle of the building. April always felt this was the most awesome room of all in the entire building. It was the middle, and you could see each room on the bottom and top floors. The ceiling looked open as you could see the sun or clouds. It had a thick glass-like covering on top. The nuns were concerned at first that the glass would break, but the contractor assured them that it was not glass. It was stronger than glass and the only concern they would have would be leaking. Each fall that ceiling was checked and if needed resealed in the time they were there. It needed sealing in two areas only, but it was good to keep it checked. They all sat down on couches or chairs in that open room. It was a room to reflect, contemplate, talk quietly, and pray.

April sat down and within minutes Mother Superior was at her shoulder. She bent over to ask April to follow her to her office. In her office Mother Superior let down much of her guard and hugged April, which surprised April to say the least. Mother Superior was quite a woman, she was firm and kind, soft and hardened, and April loved and respected her immensely.

Mother Superior sat down at her desk, removed her glasses, and wiped her eyes. She was happy, relieved, and anxious all at once. As much as she had wished for April to return, as time went on, she was doubtful. But here she was sitting right in front of her desk.

"How have you been?" Mother Superior asked April.

April looked at her and asked, "May I be completely honest and open with you - no judgments, just constructive criticism if needed?"

"Of course," Mother Superior said.

April breathed a sigh and continued. "Since my return home, my life has been chaos to say the least. I did win the farm competitions, but I lost the man I thought I would one day marry. He cheated on me with another woman, and they had a baby together. She has since left him. He has the baby with his parents while he serves in the military. I joined the military and went through a lot of hard enduring work and entered into the Frogman program. I have served one year for our government retrieving lost American soldiers being kept by foreign countries. It is dangerous, but most times, not one shot is fired. I don't love what I do. I feel I am being pulled to do it. That it is drawing me in. I was angry for a long time, but now I am doing better, being here seeing all of you makes my life better."

Mother Superior was not surprised. This one had a spirit of fire. One who was not afraid to step forth to slay dragons and lift the poor in spirit while doing so. "Are you still angry?" she asked April.

"No, not anymore. I prayed about this, and I feel as long as I am keeping the commandments and obeying the will of God, I will be all right," April told her.

"Of course," Mother Superior said to her. "That is the key. Just don't remove your eyes from the sight of your goal."

"Well, I don't really have a goal. I am there doing my job. I am no longer interested in love. I love my parents and my animals. But as far as men are concerned, that is not for me, at least not right now. Right now, I have my commitment to the US to fulfill, and so long as I live right, I will also fulfill my obligations to God," April said to her.

Mother Superior said, "We all have our own journey with trials and tribulations. Some are personal and some are for the world to see. I believe you have the strength within you to exceed your goals. I also believe you are close by our Father in Heaven. He has preserved all of us for a glorious purpose, which none of us know for sure until that moment arrives or is revealed to us," she said to April.

"Yes, I believe that too. So often we view our achievements
all in measures compared to companies and businesses, but
one the less ours are just as important," April said. "You know I
wanted to come back sooner, but there was no time, my life was
always so busy. So when I came off for leave I had this bucket list
I wanted to do, this place was one of them. I hope you forgive
me for taking so long," April said to her.

Mother Superior said, "No I cannot, for you broke my heart.
I have never met anyone like you. You give all you have without
looking back, and to someone like me, that is difficult to accept. I
wanted to hug you, hold you, and thank you, but you were gone.
I will always cherish the time we have spent together and pray for
your guidance by God. Do heed his whispers to keep safe and to
do his bidding as it pleases him. Our lives serve him," she said.

Mother Superior stood up with tears welling in her eyes,
"Now we join the others, and this conversation stays here. What I
said to you and what you said to me stays here." They stood up to
leave and April stepped forward, hugged her, and kissed her cheek
softly. Then they left her office to join the others downstairs.

The other Sisters were not down where they had left them,
so Mother Superior led the way. Then they went outside past the
flower gardens and the raised vegetable gardens to the building
at the very back of the property. Mother Superior turned the
doorknob, they stepped inside, and there greeting April were
hundreds upon hundreds of roses. Some were bushes, some
were in pots, but there were so many it was countless. There
was a long green house in the shape of the letter 'U' around
the outside of the main greenhouse which housed the young
rose bushes.

April saw a display that held a book. It was their book, showing all the kinds of roses they grew. These were for display, but they had a mailing and sent them like catalogs to order from. They found a way to support themselves. April stood there reeling with pride and love for them. What industrious, intelligent women these were. They did it. They absolutely did it.

Some of the Sisters eagerly took April around the greenhouse. They showed her how they grafted roses. April was astounded that they learned so much in such a short time and applied their talents.

April picked up one of the catalogs and leafed through the pages. There were many beautiful roses and bushes to choose from. "Send one of these to my Mom's. I will jot down their addresses. They loves flowers," she said. There were countless varieties of roses and bushes. April put the catalog back and walked outside. It was cooler here, the leaves had all turned many colors: red, orange, and yellow. Also, many of the trees were already leafless. Winter was on the way.

She walked back to the school and living quarters of the Sisters. As she stepped inside, she took a deep breath. It smelled like a school with crayons and paper. And she could imagine the many children who came on a daily basis. She sat down on a wicker chair with a cushion and laid her head back to think. April knew she could not stay very long. It was a full day's drive back and she promised her grandfather she would be there on Thursday.

As the day progressed April made clear to Mother Superior that she would not be able to stay beyond Wednesday. That gave them one day. Mother Superior understood. She knew the love this girl had for her grandfather and that she would make sure she was home in time.

The next day was filled with prayers, songs, children, laughter, and deep meaningful talks with the woman April admired deeply. She was the Mother Superior for good reason. Her heart was big, and her resolve was firm. She stood for God, Period!

Before she knew it April was packing her travel bag. She smiled as she put in the silly little cat that one of the little schoolgirls gave her. She was an imp of a child who was drawn to April. She would sit on her lap whenever she could. When the child learned April was leaving, she put this plastic cat in April's hand. Most likely it was one of her favorite toys which now belonged to April.

All packed and ready to go, it was 4 a.m. She carried her bag to the front door and waited. They were in vespers. Soon a novice noticed her and notified the others. There were a lot of hugs, blessings, and more hugs. Then she pulled her suitcase along, put it in the car, and waved goodbye.

It was almost 5 a.m. She wanted to make good time to get back to her grandparents' home. April stopped at a gas station near where she had to get on another highway. She filled the gas tank, hopped back in, buckled her seat belt, started the engine, and headed west. It was not completely light, so she flipped on her headlights. It was a nice quiet drive. There were not many cars or trucks on the road. Thankfully there was no snow on the road, and it was not windy.

April turned on the radio and listened to the local news, weather reports, and some talk show that she soon lost interest in. She turned off the radio and just drove. In her mind she was concerned about her grandfather and surmised he did not know who to call for that blessing he promised he would get. So, she mentally reminded herself to take care of that when she got in tonight.

Before long she was cruising down the highway and she knew she was about an hour away. April again turned on the radio and the Christmas songs were on every station. Then she realized it was the last week of October. In just over a week she would be returning to home base unless they called her back sooner. She instinctively touched her right pocket to feel her cell phone. Yes, it was there, and no one had called her. If they had called, the cell phone would have buzzed, so she left it in her pocket, never taking her eyes off of the road.

She had been driving five hours and April wanted to stretch her legs and walk, so she pulled off at a rest area. She went inside and used the facility, bought some bottled water and some crackers. She checked her wristwatch, it was now 8:20 a.m. she knew she had made good time and should be at her grandparents within the hour. Getting back in the car felt like a punishment. She buckled up and was on her way again. As she predicted it was 9:10 a.m. when she pulled into the back alley of her grandparents' garage.

April got out and carried her bag and jacket with her. Grandpop had been watching from the window and came out to greet her. "Oh, April, you came back," he said.

"Of course I did. I said I would," she replied to him. They went inside the home. It was nice and warm, and April could smell boiling cabbage. April put her bag back into the small room, and her grandmother was there in the small living room half asleep.

Grandmother's eyes opened slowly, and April apologized for waking her. "Would you like me to make lunch?" she asked her grandmother.

"If you can. That would be all right," her grandmother replied.

April looked in the refrigerator while her grandfather was sitting at the table reading the day's newspaper. "Psst, what do you eat with cabbage, fish or corned beef?" she asked her grandfather. He waved his hand as if to indicate either would be fine. April loved fish. She had not had any for quite some time, so she brought out the package and set it in the sink. The liquid was draining. She checked to see if the fish had been deboned, and it was.

Soon the smell of fish and cabbage filled the kitchen. April also made three small salads. She set the table and within minutes walked into the living room touching her dozing grandmother on the hand. "Dinner is ready," she said to her.

"Oh, I come," she replied to her.

It was a nice dinner, and Grandpop had a surprise too. As the dinner dishes were taken away, there was a knock on the door, and Grandpop said, "They are here." He got up to open the door. It was Tim and John with one carefully carrying something in a bag.

"What do you have there?" Grandma asked them.

"Cake," Tim said.

"Pie," John said.

"Well what is it, cake or pie?" Grandma asked.

"Both," they said grinning while setting the bag on the table.

April asked if they could have it later, as they had just finished eating dinner.

"Oh sure," the boys said.

April asked to be excused. She wanted to make a telephone call. She went into the living room and called the local bishop. She asked if there were missionaries in the area who would come to give her grandfather a blessing. He said there were not, but he would be willing to come if it was soon. He and his wife were going out of town the next morning. April said, "yes", without asking her grandparents. She hung up the telephone and walked into the kitchen to deliver the news.

No one said a word, only Grandpop "It's okay. I am here. Let them come." And they did. It was a beautiful blessing of health, caution, and to take care. It lasted less than ten minutes and soon they were sitting at the table eating pie. April thanked the two and winked at her brothers who were brimming over with questions for the bishop and his companion.

April left them to retrieve her Bible. She opened the door to the cellar and walked down the steps. She uncovered the old upright piano she had seen previously and sat down to play. Soon Grandpop was there followed by Grandma and then the two boys. Some sat on the old divan, some on chairs.

April was playing Christmas songs and singing, and they joined in. When she stopped, she asked for requests when her Grandmother asked for her to play "Silent Night". April knew this was going to be difficult as it was one of her favorite songs. She felt the depth of the words, and the discovery of the baby Jesus. She did not want to, but she always, always cried. As she played, she let go. It did not matter where she was, she was no longer in this basement, she was now in front of the scene of the Holy Child. As she played, she envisioned the entire scenario playing out before her as she played. She knew the great blessing of the birth of Jesus Christ, offering a way to live, a Savior! Yes, as she played, tears streaked down her face. Her grandmother watched her, and her eyes too had tears. After that, there were some fun songs and then April stopped.

She pulled her Bible out and read the passages in Luke telling about the birth of the Savior. This is what we call Family Home Evening. We do this every week.

The four sat there looking captivated, like this was the best thing and the most unusual thing ever. Grandpop was proud of her. She knew her scriptures and her heart was in the right place. Her grandmother was surprised. The boys were awestruck.

After the small family home evening lesson, they headed upstairs for dessert. April did not want any, but out of respect, she had a tiny piece of cake.

As they sat in the small living room, Grandpop yawned. Tim looked at his watch and said, "Oh man, we have to go. It's 7:30 already and I have to get up at 5 a.m." So the boys got their jackets and head scarves and headed out, locking the door as they left. Grandpop had already headed into his bedroom and Grandma followed. April went to her room, undressed, and showered. That warm water sure felt good after this long day, with the drive and everything. She put on her pajamas, came out, and looked around. It seemed quite enough, so she knelt down by the sofa and offered a prayer.

"Father in Heaven, I ask in the name of our Savior Jesus Christ to hear my prayer. Father, I love thee and I pray that as we go to the doctor this week that Grandpop can receive honest, intelligent, but down to earth answers. If there is a way to heal him as the blessing indicated, please Father, touch his heart to know to do whatever it takes. I am willing to do whatever it takes. I pray, Father, for mercy. Do not let him leave us so soon, me so soon. I know I was taken away for good reason, but that way also took me away from him for many, many years, and I love him." She put her head down on the couch and her tears flowed freely.

"Please, Father, thy will be done, and know that I stand by that for thou are all knowledgeable, kind, and merciful. Your plan is best. I am being greedy, Father. I know that. Forgive me, but I pray thou art being mindful of the love I have for them. I have never refused what you wanted me to do. Father, I have always trusted you. I ask this one small thing, and trust you, in the name of Jesus Christ, Amen."

As she knelt there by the sofa, she became acutely aware of someone near her, and that someone was also kneeling next to her. It was her grandmother, and her face was streaked with tears. "I pray by you too," she said. She touched April and said to her. "I did not know. April, I ask you to forgive an old foolish woman who was spiteful towards you and your Mother. I am ashamed of my hatred and ask you to forgive me. All those many years ago, I thought I could change things, but I saw I could not. Children grow and do what they want, not always what is best for them. Your father disobeyed a sacred trust of this family which I felt brought evil to us. But I see no evil in you. Having years to see what has happened, I see now your Mother was not evil, but confused and afraid. I hope one day she forgive me too. I am so sorry for all that has happened to drive you away," and she sobbed great sobs."

April could not see this and not try to comfort her. So as he put her arms around her, the old woman cried even harder and clung to April. "It's all right. Really it is. It turned out all right. No one is angry, no one is evil," she said to the old woman.

"No, no. You must understand. I was the evil one," the old woman replied to April.

"No. You were not. You wanted good for your son. You did not know the woman he married. You knew little to nothing about her, her family, or anyone else. And they did not visit you much after they married. So I understand completely how you felt. You were losing your son. Look at me. God had a plan that is all I can say. In no way did that make you evil. You are a Mother who loved her son." April felt the old woman's head nodding in affirmative.

"I worry about him too," her head motioned to their bedroom. "I don't know what I would do if I lost him. Be lost, I guess. There is no one left," her grandmother said.

"We will all cross that bridge one day. There is no sense thinking of 'what if' now," April told her.

"You smart girl. You are a blessing to us."

April could say no more. She kissed her grandmother's cheek, said "goodnight", and went to bed.

Grandmother stood there realizing it was very late. She went to bed realizing her burden had been lifted. "Yes, trust God," she said silently and soon her contented heart left her sleep.

In the morning, breakfast was simple oatmeal and fruit. Then they all dressed to go to the doctor. April insisted she take her car since the gas tank was full. It struck her odd that they both climbed into the back seat, as if she were the chaffier.

The trip was about forty five minutes. The traffic was not bad, but it was the office that was difficult to find. It was located in a big complex of other offices. April asked them to wait, so she could go inside to be sure it was the right office. As she came out, she had a parking sticker that permitted them to park for free. They all walked in together, taking their time since they were twenty minutes early. They sat down in the office, Grandpop stepped to the receptionist to tell her his name, and then sat down.

Not much was said. Soon he was called and the three of them followed a nurse to the room. The nurse checked his blood pressure, pulse, and then said the doctor would be in shortly. She closed the door as she left.

"They busy putting peoples into rooms," Grandpop chuckled.

"Yes, they are. I bet they see sixty or more in a day," April said.

As the doctor entered the room, he looked oddly at April, but continued to speak to Grandpop. He told Grandpop he had ulcers, and if not careful to eat a bland diet they were likely to bleed, which would lead to a mired of other problems. Grandpop asked if there was a chart of foods he could eat. "Well that's sort of a no brainer" the doctor rudely said. April held her tongue. "Am I to go on medication?" Grandpop asked. "Well, no. Not at this time. We will wait and see how changing the food goes. If you have more problems, we will think about medication then."

Now April was getting angry.

"So you do not believe in preventive medication?" April questioned the doctor.

"Well no, not unless there is an obvious problem," he said back to her.

"You don't consider an ulcer a problem?" April asked.

"Yes and no," the doctor began.

April was putting on her jacket, "Come on, Grandpop. He is not interested in healing you. I can get you more help than he is offering."

"Hold on a minute," the doctor said. "He is my patient. You can't just walk out like that."

Grandpop looked at him and said, "We go. Not your patient no more. Goodbye. Have a nice day," and they were out of there.

In the car April pulled out her cell phone and called her doctor in California, asking him questions. He referred her to see another doctor that was close by and highly recommended.

Her doctor told her he would make the call himself, explain that we were nearby, and have her Grandpop seen today. April sat in the car waiting.

"You know people," Grandpop said.

"Well, yeah. I don't believe any doctor worth his salt would wait until you had a problem worse than it is now." Soon her cell phone rang. It was the new office calling. They were two buildings over, could work Grandpop in, and could just come on over.

This office was friendly, not over worked. The nurse was very kind and talked as she checked Grandpop's blood pressure. Within minutes, before the nurse was done, the doctor entered the room. He spoke candidly with them. He answered all of their questions. He felt that after he changed his diet, then he would order some scans. But for now, he suggested Grandpop try a bland diet that the nurses would give him with a menu plan. And he encouraged Grandpop to take an antacid pill that can be purchased over the counter. After the scans, if needed, he would call them with further instructions. And if Grandpop needed to be on a prescription medication, he could call it in to a local pharmacy for them. He left thanking them for coming in.

"What a difference," Grandma said as they all put on their jackets. Grandpop was silent. He looked at April and winked at her. He knew she had pull, and if she was in his corner, he would be all right. On their way out they indeed got sheets of appropriate fruits and vegetables, menu ideas, and so on for Grandma to change their diet, but not so drastically. On the way home April said they would stop for lunch and try out a bland menu. They did and Grandpop thought it would be terrible, but it was not so bad after all. "I can live with this," he thought. But he said, "April, you're all right."

The next day Grandpop wanted to go for a ride, so they all piled into his car with him driving. April gave him a small plastic bottle of antacid pills that made a world of a difference. He stopped burping and no more burning in his stomach.

He drove to where he had farmed. Little remained. The barn had been revamped into a business and the house was gone. As they entered the lane it all was familiar to April. In her mind she could still see the house where it stood, the stone walkway, and the flowers that lined the steps. As they walked the new owner and manager of the shop came out. They talked and he told them to go wherever they wanted. Out beyond where the house had stood, the trees still were there, and the old rope swing with the board that Grandpop used to swing her was still there. "You want me to push you, April," Grandpop teased her.

"I would, but I am a few pounds heavier now," she teased him right back. Grandpop put his arm around her, they walked all around, and then back to the barn.

The original barn was still there including the top, where the shop was located to store their equipment and work on things. Grandpop led April to the steps that went down. "Do you remember this?" and he pointed to an etching that had been made long ago with a pocketknife. It had April's name on it in a heart. "You were my little girl," Grandpop said with a sniff. He reached for the hanky in his pocket. April ran her hand over the name and realized she had been too young to have made this. She knew beyond any doubt that her Grandpop had loved her since she was a tiny little girl.

They soon left and Grandpop headed in another direction. This drive was about a half hour and as he drove up the dirt road April felt her skin crawl. "Oh please don't take me here," she said to him. "It has been mostly all bad memories here, and I never wanted to come back."

Grandpop did not listen to her. He acted as if he had not heard her. He parked the car and opened the back door where April was sitting. "You come. I be with you," he said to her.

They stood there for quite a long time April building her nerve, taking in buildings, and remembering. She could still recall some of the awful things that had happened to her. "It is good to face our fears and conquer them, no?" Grandpop said.

April took a big breath and began to walk. She walked up the cement steps to the house, and she felt her otherwise strong legs, buckle. Grandpop held onto her arm for support. The house was empty, for sale, and no one lived there.

They entered the mud room where they hung all of their coats and removed their muddy boots. It was also where April received hundreds of strappings by her Daddy's belt. Next into the kitchen where she hid under the telephone cabinet to escape him. It also was where Mother would spend hours cooking and baking. Often giving April the beaters and bowl to lick.

Into the dining room where she remembered eating her dinner on the floor under the table, while her father screamed and ranted at her or her Mother. To the living room where her Dad was king, and no one dare speak to him while he was watching TV or reading the newspaper. She stopped at the parlor door. She did not want to do in because it was there she had to lean over a chair for spankings and her legs and butt would be bloody with welts.

Upstairs was not so bad, she remembered where everyone slept, and she absolutely refused to go into the basement. She vowed never to step inside that death place ever again. It was here her father tortured her beloved pets. He would kill them in front of her for her punishment when she did not listen. He was a cruel, sick, twisted man, and she did not ever want to be in his life again.

Grandpop had tears in his eyes, "I did not know, April. I came every day, and I suspected but when I asked, he lied, and I did not know."

"I don't blame you, Grandpop, or you either Grandma. I understand that when someone grows up, they are responsible for their own decisions and actions. What he did, he did alone, to me and my brothers. He made his bed, and he will sleep in it too. I don't believe Tim or John will bother with him anymore, and I certainly will not. The only thing that bothers me is I must forgive him someday, but for now I just can't. What he did to me was heinous, cruel, and criminal.

They walked outside and April remembered the many dogs that had lived in the dog house. Some her father shot, and some he dragged to their death. April had tears in her eyes remembering. Then to the barn where many of her beloved ponies had lived. She ran her hand along the top rail remembering them. She remembered sitting in the calf pen while her Mother milked. The barn had not changed, not much at all. She remembered on bone chilling mornings when the temperatures dipped below zero, the barn was cozy and warm. Yes, she loved the barn much more than she ever did that house. As she stood there realizing! She realized it was because "he" never came into the barn. The barn was Mother's refuge.

As they stood there, Grandpop said, "I bought this farm for my son. I thought this would be a good place, but it ended up turning into a place of hell," and he began to walk out.

Soon they were standing outside in the tractor cove right beside the barn. The winds had picked up and it was downright cold. "I am not sure what the temperature is, but it sure is chilly," she said. She tugged on her Grandpop's arm. "What you did was a generous thing out of kindness. Never regret that. What HE did was out of your control. He was at the helm of his life, and the lives of his wife and children. HE was the one who messed up, messing up everyone else. You did not do anything wrong. HE did," she told him.

"I know April, but it does not make me feel any better. I see the pain in you and your brothers, and it is not right," he replied. Grandma was crying, so they all got into Grandpop's car, blew their noses, and got warm.

They headed out even further west this time to stop for dinner. "Okay," April said. "But this is my treat." Grandma winked at her. She liked this spunky young woman. She had a good heart and was usually cheerful.

She did not know about all those years, or the problems with her son, but she believed him. Now she and her husband had to live with the regret of what had happened.

April put her arm around her waist. "Don't cry over spilt milk," ever hear of that?" April asked her.

"Yes. Yes, I have," she said shaking her head.

April then said, "Let the past stay in the past. It's long over. We are all healing, and happy now."

"Yes," she said, and they entered the restaurant.

This was a local favorite. They came from miles and miles around because they were known for their home baked goods and ice cream. They all ordered their dinners and Grandpop made another good choice in bland foods. "It's not so hard," he said almost half laughing.

They ate and left. April also picked up two quarts of ice cream for her grandparents to enjoy when she left. Then on the way out, grandmother told April she was spoiling her. She had not made dinner for two days now.

"Well it's good to go out every now and then. It's a break in day-to-day life. Don't you agree? And I have not had a chance to spoil you two in many years."

Her grandmother said, "Yes, but I like to cook. I not so used to going out. They all got in Grandpop's car and headed for home. It was going on dusk, but they were home and safe before dark.

They were tired from all the traveling. April was exhausted from going to what she called the "Hell House". She vowed never to go there again. If she had her way that house would be bulldozed down. She had no intention of doing anything like that. She did not want to live here, and the land had been divided up and sold for house lots. Nope she loved where she grew up.

Grandpop turned on the news to catch the weather and there was a storm coming. The station was not sure how much snow would fall, but somewhere between two and ten inches. "That's a big stretch," Grandpop said. April told him if that much fell she would love to shovel it. They do not get snow in California. But as it was it was a mere two inches that blew away in the winter winds.

April was relaxed. She enjoyed this old couple's company, and wished they would, "come to her home". All they had were each other and this home. Sure they had friends, but friends come and go. There are churches everywhere, but all she could do was make suggestions.

As the days passed April knew she had to say goodbye to these two, as much as she hated to. She did make clear to them that anytime they needed anything at all, just call her Dad, or Mr. Stevens.

The night before she left, they sat down together in the small living room, April handed each of them a bowl of popcorn. "No salt, just a scant bit of butter," she said. As they sat there April told them about where she would be during the next year to year and a half. "You both know I am in the military, and I am not sure where I will be. I cannot write about what I did. I am often in foreign countries and am not able to write or call." Grandpop looked at her and could not fathom what this young girl had seen and been through. He surmised that growing up hard probably prepared her for active duty. He knew she was mentally tough and physically strong, but her heart was tender.

A lot was said, and many questions asked and answered. April was open about her personal life as well. That night in bed, Grandma asked her husband "Do you think she will be in danger and could be killed?"

"Yes," he said. "That is possible." Grandma turned on her side and felt tears run onto her pillow. She did not want any harm to come to her, but this was her life. All she could do is pray for her. As she lay there, she felt her husband arm slip around her.

Neither of them slept well that night. They both were unsettled thinking she volunteered to go on dangerous missions.

As Grandpop sat at the kitchen table, he believed that it was good. This girl was a fighter for good. She was valiant to serve her country and to rescue people in order to bring them home to their families. Yes, she was brave, strong, and had her mind made up. He understood what she meant when she said, "pulled to it". He knew because long ago when he left his native country, he felt pulled to come to America. It was something inherit within him. He just knew he had to do it. He understood.

Her grandparents knew April would be leaving soon. They were happy she was able to stay as long as she had.

The telephone rang loud, and Grandpop answered it. "Hold on," he said. Then he got up and walked to the room where April was packing. "Telephone for you," he said.

April came out and the telephone and cord was lying on the kitchen table. She picked it up and said, "Hello?"

"Hello, April. This is Dr. Marcus. You were in recently with your grandparents?"

"Yes. I remember you," April said.

"Well, I was wondering if you would like to go out for dinner with me?" he asked.

April felt bad. She knew what was going on, but it was okay. She also knew she had to go and be back. Immediately April said to him, "I appreciate this. I really do, but I am home on leave from active duty. I have to report back, and I leave tonight."

"Oh, wow! I have bad timing. don't I?" the doctor said. "Well how is your grandfather doing with that bland diet?"

"Oh, pretty well actually. We went out to eat and his choices were wise. I believe the both of them will work on it together, and I also want to thank you for taking Grandpop in when you did. It was very kind of you," she said.

"Yes, well, Okay. Well, I had better be going. And stay in touch if you can. I would love to see you sometime," he concluded, and the call ended.

Grandpop was eager to know what was said. "Not much really," April told him.

"April, you going to be old maid," he said laughing. April rolled her eyes and laughed too.

Soon she was packing up and heading out the door. She kissed them both, waved goodbye, and was soon traveling on the interstate to the airport. On the way she put a call into Mr. Stevens asking that their small airplane meet her there. She did not know how to get the car back and Mr. Stevens said he would send someone along on the flight to drive the car back.

Headed Back Home

So there she was waiting on the tarmac for their twin Cessna to come in. She did not have to wait long. She saw the red on the wings come taxing down the runway. April waiting until the Cessna came to a halt along the side of the hangar. Their pilot, Scott, got out, removed his sunglasses, and zipped up his jacket. "It sure is cold here. How are you pumpkin?" he teased April.

"I am okay. Wanting to get home if that's all right with you?"

"You're the boss. Let me stretch my legs for a few minutes," and he was off to talk to some of the crew at the hangar. The guy he brought along was about nineteen. He was more than happy to drive back to California. April showed him where the car was and handed him the keys. He saluted her and left.

When Scott came back, he looked at April and asked, "Are you ready?"

"Yes, Sir. I am," she replied. The pilot gave the tower coordinates and waited their turn to taxi down the runway and fly home.

As they sat in line, April put on the other headset. "You want to fly her," Scott asked.

"Nope. I just want to sit here and enjoy the flight. You're an awesome pilot," he just laughed. He tapped on his headset he did that when he was waiting, sort of a nervous twitch. Soon the tower radioed them to go and go they did. April never got over the thrill of lift off. It made her smile.

The flight was uneventful, and they could visually see falling snow in parts of the country. They were back in Fresno in four hours. Sure was faster than driving. He showed April there was a truck waiting for her. As she approached the truck, she looked at her watch. It was almost 1 p.m. She would have ten days and five hours to spend here with her parents and those whom she knew best.

April started the truck's engine. It turned over easily. She turned to head for home. She enjoyed the trip and drove slowly. She remembered every hill, their slope, and every tree. It was so good to be home.

As she pulled into the driveway, she parked down at the barn as she always had. In minutes Ruby came over barking at her. "Are you barking at me?" she asked the dog. Ruby stopped barking and began to cry for April to pay attention to her or pick her up. "You're out of luck, girl. You are all full of mud and Mom's not going to like that." She ruffled her head and said, "Come on." Then they headed to the house.

Miranda was watching from the window. It was so typical. April was here and then she was gone. But she figured it was that way for everyone. Children are not yours. They will one day go off on their own and make a life for themselves. It was not easy, but that is how it is meant to be, she surmised. She opened the door for April and a very muddy Ruby. "Will you please put her in the laundry room until I can clean her up?" she asked her daughter.

"I'll do it," April said.

That was another thing. No matter the animal, if it needed help, she would always stop and help it. She was so known for being late to meetings or events. Miranda sighed. She would not want her daughter to be any different.

April carried a wet but clean Ruby out in a towel, and she reached to hug her Mother with one arm. "Gosh it's good to be back," April said.

"Can you sit down and tell me what your trip was like?" her Mother inquired. They sat down at the kitchen table and like two women and old friends they sat and talked. The entire trip was covered in less than an hour. Miranda made some comments, and had some questions, which were all answered. It was so wonderful to have a relationship with a mature daughter who was open and honest with her. There was nothing they could not talk about. They trusted each other.

As they talked Miranda asked April if she would be willing to sing again for Christmas. "Oh, Mom. I am here for ten odd days, and I don't really want to sing. I have not sung for two years, not like it was when I was in High School."

"I think you should pray about it," her Mother replied.

"So what are your plans?" April asked her Mother.

"My plans?" Miranda restated.

"Oh, Mom, for heaven's sakes. You plan everything. When are Manny and the family coming and Lena and June. I want to spend time with all of you," April said to her Mother.

"Well, I invited them all to the Town Christmas Program and had hoped you would sing. April felt resigned. She could not win. Her Mother had good intentions, but April did not want to shine. Let someone else do it. There surely was someone who WANTED to sing.

Her Mom planned dinner but needed a few things. April said she would drive into town, see her Dad and the Ladies, and then pick up what her Mom wanted. So April left. She pulled down the street a bit so her Dad would not see her coming. She walked up the street and opened the door. Dad was busy reading a report. April put her finger to her lips so Randy would not say anything. She walked to the door frame and knocked. Gordon looked up and sprang from his desk to embrace his daughter. They talked eagerly for about fifteen minutes, when April told him she had to get some things from the store for dinner.

She went to the Ladies' home, and by luck they were loading their car to go cleaning. As she pulled up to the garage, she parked just letting enough room for them to pull out. As suspected, one came out to see who had the nerve to park them in. It was June. She did not return to help her sister load the car, so Lena came out to see why. Then she knew. The three of them talked outside, and April helped them load their car. They had landed a contract with an office. There were six of them in all, so they did them all on Friday night. This was the night. April told them to go, and she would see them real soon. They hugged her and they regrettably left waving out their windows.

April went to the store and picked up the three items Miranda wanted and then she picked up some things for a sauce that was awesome for hotdogs or hamburgers. Here is the recipe for you!

Nick's and her Mom's sauce
2 pounds hamburger
20 ounces ketchup
1/2 teaspoon turmeric
1 teaspoon dry mustard
1/3 teaspoon ground cloves

1 teaspoon cinnamon

1 teaspoon chili powder

1 teaspoon pepper

2 teaspoons sea salt

Fry and drain hamburger. Add all other ingredients and mix. Let simmer until it thickens. Delicious on hamburgers or hot dogs.

Crock Pot Baked Beans

1 pound hamburger

1/4 pound good bacon

1 cup chopped onions

1 #2 bush baked beans

1 #2 can chili beans (hot)

1 #1 can baby lima beans & juice from can

1 cup ketchup

1/4 cup brown sugar

1 tablespoon liquid smoke

3 tablespoon white vinegar

1 tablespoon sea salt

April rolled into her driveway with Christmas songs blaring. As she grabbed the bag of groceries and entered her home, her Mom was on the telephone. "Hold on. She is standing right her," and Miranda handed April the telephone.

April covered the receiver and asked, "Who is this?" Miranda acted like she did not know. A little irritated April put the receiver to her ear and said, "Hello?"

"Hello, April. How are you?"

By golly it was Mrs. Walker. April had not seen her since the flower show so long ago. "Hello, Mrs. Walker. How are you?" April asked.

"Well, I am calling to ask you, April, if you would be kind enough to sing at the Community Center Christmas Party? It's being held in the park."

April grimaced. In her sweetest voice April asked, "Isn't there someone else who wants to do it?"

"Well", Mrs. Walker hesitated. "There is, but she is new to our town. And well, she doesn't sing well."

April felt trapped. "Well then, I would love to do it, but can a choir sing with me?" she whole heartedly asked. Miranda's heart swelled. "We should practice though don't you think so?" April asked Mrs. Walker.

"Yes. We will be rehearsing twice, two days before the event. Just come down to the park about 2 p.m. I am thrilled you have consented to sing and help us out. Everyone knows you and it will be lovely," Mrs. Walker said.

April hung up the phone feeling like she was defeated. She gathered up her old friend who liked her no matter what, and who would defend her from strangers or uniforms with all of her six pounds. She pulled her onto the couch and talked to her.

"Don't go spoiling her. When you go, we have to deal with her," Miranda hollered to her. "Awe Mom, I won't" April said.

April looked into Ruby's eyes. She was getting old, but she still had that spark in her eyes. She loved her and would give April her soul. All she wanted was love, a little bit of food and water, and shelter. She always gave back one hundred times what you gave her in love. Ruby laid on her body with her paws near her neck, and her face next to hers. She panted and with the slightest move of April's eyes, she would become excited. April was grateful that Dad loved Ruby too. Dad knew Ruby needed to be needed, and he gladly took April's place as best as he could with Ruby.

April fell asleep. She dreamed and, in that dream, she saw men, a lot of men, climbing hills, looking in woods, and searching. For what, she did not know. They made calls, drove looking and looking. It was confusing to her. It made no sense and left her tired. But she knew not to ignore dreams. Often thing you need to know later are revealed in dreams. It happened like that before for her, but she wondered where she was while they were searching.

She was glad it was 5:30 p.m. Dad would be home. Dinner was always delicious, and she felt a slight pang of guilt. She slept and had not helped. She enjoyed the day-to-day things, the talk at the table, laughing and catching up on things in the community and with people. That is what she missed most.

"Did you know Hugh made Captain?" her Dad asked her at the supper table.

"Yes, I knew that. I ran into him recently," she replied. She did not tell them the whole truth. What was the point?

She learned much had been added at the park, a community center. The people of the town and out in the country wanted it. They had auctions there of all sorts. It had a nice pavilion on the back for family reunions and picnics. April said when she went to practice, she would see it. Dinner was finished and April helped to clean up. The dishwasher was loaded, and they all sat in the living room.

"I want to tell you about the Community Christmas," her Mother said. "There is going to be sleigh rides by Santa Claus," and she nodded at Dad. April laughed slapping her forehead. "There will be a lot of food, from finger foods to big meal food. All of it is being volunteered, there will be pasta dishes, a lot of vegetables. The town chose to roast a pig on a spit, and of course there will be hot dogs and hamburgers. The mothers of the 4H are bringing in brownies, cakes, and pies. I think everything is covered," she said proudly. "The High School band is playing, and we have a group coming in to play bells. That should be lovely."

"The scouts are escorting anyone who might have trouble, and our police department is bringing people into the Center with four-wheelers pulling a wagon, low enough to sit on, and hopefully they will go slow."

"Wow! Seems like you have it all covered." April teased her.

"All but someone to sing," her Mother said, and April threw a small pillow at her which Ruby began to bark defensively at Miranda. "See what you did?" Miranda said to April. "Come here, Ruby" Miranda coaxed, but the little dog stood faithfully at April's side. April coaxed Ruby to be quiet.

"So what song do you want to sing?" Miranda asked her daughter.

April gleefully looked at her Mother and said, "Grandma got run over by a reindeer."

Gordon laughed and Miranda's eyes scowled. "Your family will all be there, April!" She knew her daughter was having fun at her expense, but she had to pick a song. "Mom, don't be so serious. I will choose a song and try not to embarrass you," April said.

"Oh, come on now. You have never embarrassed me. We have always been so proud of you, dear."

That was enough, April got up and walk to her Mom, "Mom, I was just razzing you. I am sorry," and hugged her Mother.

The next several days were visiting, visiting, and more visiting. She practiced the song, "Hark the Herald Angels Sing" with the choir. Her mother was sure April had something warm to wear, a red wool skirt and cape to match, and she still had her old boots. This winter was chilly. Everyone was wearing a jacket and cap or beanie, and she was grateful she had warm clothing even though she lived in California.

One morning very early April escaped. She took the old pickup truck and headed to the stable where Native Son was still servicing mares.

She pulled into the driveway, headed into the barn, and was greeted by Bo, the half Australian shepherd. April entered the barn and the barn swallows swooped at her warning to let their nests alone.

As she walked through the barn, she heard nickers as the horses greeting her, and then there was the undeniable familiar whinny of the only male who never disappointed her. There he was in his grandeur. Native Son had put on weight, but his coat was sleek and shiny. His head was refined and grand. She ran to him, opened his stall gate, threw her arms around him, and stood there for a long, long time. Native Son would have been content to stand there for as long as she needed. There was no denying he loved her, he knew her, he felt her pain and sadness as well as her joy and love. He was older, but still spry enough to race and do well. April spent the afternoon with him. It was such a little time with the one who propelled so many out of poverty and desperation. When she left him, she rubbed his head and gave him a carrot, still his favorite.

Monte was there but left her alone. From time to time he would swear that Native Son was depressed. He was a good horse, never made trouble, and serviced mares very business-like. But occasionally he would stare out his window, look for something, and never gave up. Monte asked Miranda for a picture of April. Miranda agreed and Monte took it to a place to make a stuffed doll that looked like April. He put the doll in the stall and once in a while Native Son would nudge the doll or stand there beside it. Monte swore that the doll helped the horse.

One day while in town, April went through the city park and was amazed at how well her last request turned out. The proposal was to raise money and not taxes for this project. Residents could purchase a brick for three dollars and have their initials on it. For five dollars the families' name and year would be added to the brick. They were also available to single folks as well.

As April walked through the park, the bricks bore so many names she knew. She found herself walking with her head down discovering names. There was also a lovely fountain with running water, and more bricks with names cascading down on both sides. You would think being all brick it would be cold, but on the contrary, it was bright and lovely. April smiled from ear to ear as she sat there. This was awesome and indeed she was pleased.

April spent several days with her Mother and Lena. They visited and talked. June showed April how to make her coveted nut rolls. Everyone loved them. She told April she could have sold the recipe but chose not to. April being the generous soul that she was she wanted the recipe to be for everyone to enjoy. A rich nutty roll sweet and delicious, a wonderful addition to any Christmas table.

Nora June's Nut Roll

(In 1963 she was offered $500 by a baking company for this recipe, but she declined. It was her creation. Now I am sharing it with those who love these books.)

½ pound of margarine or butter   1 small yeast cake

3 eggs   1 TBsp sugar

3 cups of flour

Combine in a large bowl   ½ cup of rum or cream

Margarine, eggs, and flour

In a separate small bowl dissolve the small yeast cake and 1 Tablespoon of sugar in a ¼ cup of warm water. Then add the ½ cup of rumor cream. Add this mix to the flour. Mix well adding flour as needed. Knead until soft and smooth.

Divide flour mix into 5 balls. Roll out on crushed graham crackers and confectioner sugar, it should be a light brown color and crumbly. Turn the dough over to be completely covered in crumb mix

This is the filling: 1 pound of finely ground English walnuts. (we like black walnuts best)

Then put in 1 teaspoon of cinnamon, I cup of sugar, milk or rum, just enough to have the walnut filling to spread.

Roll up like a jelly roll and bake 350 for 20 to 25 minutes. Do not overfill with walnut spread or they will split. You can back as many as 3 to 4 at a time.

Honestly this is great at Easter or Christmas, a wonderful addition to any table setting. With much love for all those who purchase this book!

As they worked together, she and her birth Mother talked about many things, April's hopes, dreams, and aspirations. For some reason her birth Mother was easier to talk to than the Mother who raised her. She had much less rules and less expectations but inspired her to do all she could.

They talked about love, marriage, and things girls want to know. "But how do you know if you love someone. I mean really love them?" April asked her.

"Well, if they were hurt in an accident, would you be willing to take care of them for the rest of their life. Not be angry, and still be kind and loving to them?" That was eye opening to April. "If you have good to do, let that good be to your partner. Always work to love them, with notes and flowers."

April wrinkled her nose.

"Yes, Dear. Men do like flowers. Take them to places they like and some you like mutually. Marriage takes work. It is not one sided. That is what happened to me. Everything became his way or no way, and I just could not bear the beatings anymore. He was angry all the time. Nothing pleased him. And, well, with you gone, I realized soon all of the children would be gone and it would be him and me. And I could no longer get away from him. I had to leave."

"Sadly, my sister was in the same predicament. So, when Lena called me crying, she had to get away. We just prayed and reached out to your parents, Gordon and Miranda. They accepted us. They helped us in every way. I was not so sure in the beginning, but, April, they held nothing against us. They welcomed us in like family. Something I had not felt or experienced in a long, long time. You, my Dear, have had an excellent example of what a marriage should be. Your parents are close and always helping each other. I imagine you don't always see them, but we do, and we are so happy for them. It gives us hope.

You see we love each other like sisters. When she calls me, I listen and lift her, and she helps me. But neither of us want to go through the rest of our lives alone, without a companion. But if that man does not accept us as sisters, needing to be with one another, he is the wrong man. Can you understand that?"

April did, she hugged her Mother and kissed her cheek. "Thanks. It's a lot to take in. Men are to try to obey the commandments and live the way Jesus taught. They should treat women as their companions and love them. Women are to live the same way, and it is right for them to live submissive and obey their husband. So long as they agree on what they are doing or discussing things positively. That is what I hope for, Mom."

"Knowing you as I do, I believe you. Do not settle, April. Always strive for what you want." She hugged her daughter and went about making more nut rolls for the Christmas celebration.

Yes, the ten odd days went very fast. April could not believe it as she marked each day in a big "X" on the calendar in her bedroom.

The Community Christmas was wonderful. The borough put up lights in the park that twinkled. They also had candles on each light pole in town. The Community Center was a big place, considering the outside and the building. The building was open for the Christmas celebration, filled with all sorts of food that was kept warm with crock pots or small burners. Her Dad was giving hayrides and the Sheriff's department brought cart load after cart load to the Center. Most folks wanted to walk, but for families chasing after little children or for elderly, the carts were such a good idea.

The High School band played many Christmas songs while people milled around meeting one another or enjoying the many vendors that were there with displays of things for sale. That was the only money involved should you want to buy something, but the food and drink were provided free.

At 6:30 the festivities really began. There were songs, a flute presentation, a bell choir, a children's choir, a small puppet show, and then it was April's turn to sing with the choir. Some people clapped when her name was called because they knew her. As she sang, she was not nervous. She felt confident and put forth the sweetest musical notes with her voice. She saw her parents standing together holding hands. She also saw many people she knew, and then she saw the Marshalls with their grandson. He was growing so big. He was able to walk, and his Grandpa had to hold him so he would not wander off.

She let the words overtake her and transcend her to a place that only the song could fill. The choir did an awesome job, better than in practice. When she was done, everyone clapped and some whistled. She just wanted to get off the stage.

As April came down to her parents, the Marshalls were with them including Hugh and Trevor. Talk about awkward. April stood with her parents and made small talk with them. As outgoing as she was, small talk was difficult. It was Hugh that approached April. He was jovial and very kind. April was receptive but cautious, under the watchful eye of Elaine Marshall. So the seven of them talked for a while, then decided to go and get something to eat.

April watched over her shoulder. She hoped her Mom was right behind her, but it was Hugh. He was talking to others nearby in the line and occasionally taking some spoonsful of food. April made herself busy looking at the different foods. She was putting one tablespoon only of each on her plate and moved on. She stood at the pig spit and asked for a rib. "Only one rib?" the Bob asked her. April smiled as Bob cut off a good six-inch slice of ribs for her. "Where are ya sitting, Darling, and I will carry it over to the table for you."

"Ah, with my parents. Wherever they are," April said.

When Hugh leaned over and said, "I can take it for her. She is sitting with us," and so Hugh carried her plate to a spot for her and left to get his own things. April was confused. She felt trapped and did not like that. But part of her liked his attention, if only he had not done what he did to her. April let it go and soon her Mother and the Ladies were sitting on both sides of her. She felt this was a safer distance from Hugh.

Hugh sat down right across from April and was joined by his parents and brother. He put little Michael on his lap. Her Dad came in from giving the horse some hay for the night. He had his plate brimming. "Oh, Gordon, did you have to take so much. I mean look at your plate. You don't have to be so greedy. There are a lot of people here," Miranda said.

"Oh, it's okay, Honey. I told them this plate was for you," Gordon teased. Miranda was a bit flustered. It was so like her husband to tease her. They were all together and Lena took the lead and said a prayer over their food. They had a good time. The baby's face wrinkled at the taste of some of the foods, which made everyone laugh, including April. At one of those moments Hugh looked up and stared at April.

Oh how she wished someone would come along and ask her to do something, or maybe she could get up and go to the bathroom. Then Diane came by. She had been in April's graduating class. She had enlisted in the Air Force and wanted to talk. April wanted to kiss her for the excuse to leave. They found a corner seat on a bench and talked town talk. April caught up on a lot of "couples" news since leaving.

"Are you with Hugh?" Diane asked.

"No. I am not," April told her. "When Hugh cheated on me while I was away, I no longer trust him. I would never have cheated on him while he was in the military, and I don't want a man I need to worry about," April told her.

"Wow! You sure have your mind made up then? You would mind if he and I went out to see if we hit it off? I mean we are both military" Diane said.

"By all means. Go ahead and have fun," April told her and hugged the girl.

As the girls walked back to the table, Hugh was gone. It seems it was bedtime for little Michael. Diane was disappointed. She only had three more days leave. April encouraged her to call the Marshalls' home and talk with Hugh.

April felt this night was like a dream – the lights, folks she had not seen in a long while, her parents, the Ladies, and Grandpa Manny and Contessa with their entourage all came. It was really nice. She even danced a couple of dances with some guys she knew. By 10, she was tired, and the Ladies drove her home to stay with them overnight.

April slept but was up by 5:00 a.m. She made breakfast for the Ladies who protested because they usually only had tea and toast in the morning. Since they were good sports and kind, they ate the omelets April had made.

April felt such a deep love for these two women, and realized they were her past, her genealogy, and their blood was in her. "You both know I will not be home for Christmas," April stated to them.

"You won't? That's a shame, but it will give us more time to shop. What do you want this year?" they asked her.

April thought a minute and said, "If anything, I would like my family history from the two of you, from you to as far back as you can remember. I would love to have their names, relationships, years born, married, died, and what they did for a living. I would like the information for all of them: cousins, aunts, and uncles, any hobbies, and where they lived. So this will cost you nothing but racking your brains and a few phone calls." Their eyes were wild with ideas, and they began to chat like squirrels. "You see, I didn't know any of them, so any information you can give to me will mean so much to me," April said to them.

"Awe, we can do this. It will take some time, but we will get it done for you. And besides, it will be a lot of fun to talk to relatives who live up north in Michigan and down south in Florida. It might even require a road trip," and they laughed. Watching them, April wished she had a sister, someone close to her to share things with. These two were the epitome of sisters. That is what they should be, always accepting, always supportive, always love for one to another.

They spent two days together, driving around, showing April where they worked. She met some of their friends at an impromptu party at their home. It was lovely, all of it. April knew it would be difficult to say goodbye to them.

But the time came, and they all had tears. April wiped their cheeks and said, "Don't cry, this is just 'see ya later', you know? There is no other place I would rather be than here at home. You both know that."

"Yes. We know, but we miss you so much and we worry about you. You are so fearless, and we want you to take care," they said to April.

"For now that is my job. Daring I guess you'd call it, but I do it for my country and I never go without having prayer," she said.

They dropped her off at her parent's home on Sunday afternoon after church. Her Mom and Dad had just gotten home from services too. They looked so happy to see them. "I have a nice pan of lasagna in the oven. Please stay for lunch," Miranda said to them.

The Ladies always felt like they were intruding. They had not brought along anything to contribute to the meal.

"Oh, nonsense," Miranda said. "Here. Help make the salad. That would be a big help," and they did.

It was a nice meal. April liberally talked about going back. She was sure she would go on more missions. She had another year and then she was out. But that would have to wait and see. They all were anxious for her to come back home SAFE!

"What are your plans while I am gone?" April asked them.

Dad spoke first. "Well, I have my job, the Ladies work almost every day, and Mom still takes care of the farm. She feeds the ponies and keeps the riders going on weekends. She also manages the rentals and keeps me on track, so there are no big plans here that I know of," he said.

"Well" Lena spoke up. "We might take that trip to Michigan and Florida to get some family history, you know. Or maybe we would travel up North, but that would not be for more than two weeks. We know we would be welcome, and it would be nice for them to know about you, April."

Miranda and Gordon did not know about this and asked.

"Well. We thought that April would like her family history. There are many good people in her line, and she should know them, who they were, how she is related, what they did for a job, who they married, children, and so on. It's quite fascinating. We know there were many Marx women in our family. Long before television, it was common for shooters to come to towns and charge money to watch their shooting skills, like Annie Oakley. One of April's great aunts was in Africa doing such a show when her mother was found frozen in the water and mud. It happened after checking her trap lines the day before. She was in her 80s. She had an accident out on the water and got her hand stuck in a steel trap. She could not release the trap, so she rowed her boat home, got out of the boat, got stuck in the mud, froze, and died there."

Miranda's jaw dropped, "Absolutely, do her family history. It is obvious she follows that line," and they all laughed.

Then the conversation switched to a more serious tone. "April, what do you plan to do when you are out of the service?"

"Well, Dad. I would still like to go to school, maybe vet school. I could be of use on the farms or even on the tracks. I can't race horses for the rest of my life." April said. "I have some time to think about it. I will not leave before I spend some time here at home though. I kind of like it here."

"You know you can enter your own program and go to school that way," Dad said.

"I know, Dad, but I want to get done. I have paid my dues, so to speak. If I could, I would like to take an accelerated program and finish in four years. That would be sweet," April said.

"Don't be in such a rush to get done. Taking time for hands-on learning makes a world of difference," June said.

"Here, here. I agree," Miranda said. "That is so like her though. Like a bull pushing right through to get things done, and sometimes leaving collateral damage."

April was shocked, "I have not done that!"

"You have too," her Dad said. "Look around this table. You broke all of our hearts when you entered the military. We all were heart broken. Your decisions will always affect us, all of us, including Manny, Contessa, all of your cousins, your grandparents, and brothers in the East. Yes, we all now see why you went and by the Grace of God thankfully he protected you. We were wrong to take it so personally, but even the good you did. We all served with you. Do you understand that?" Dad inquired.

He was right, what could she say? April just put her silverware down, looked around the table with tears in her eyes, and thanked them. It was a very moving experience that bound their hearts even closer. April now knew how blessed she was to have people love and care for her. She saw many soldiers who did not. Never again would she take this lightly. She wanted them to know she loved them too and told them so.

Dishes were in the dishwasher, and the Ladies left about 4:00. There were chores to be done, and April and her parents rode the four-wheeler around to the farms. It was nice to see them working and everyone getting along so well. They came home and fed the ponies. Dobbins sure was grey, but always knew April. April had six more days left, six, and she knew they would fly by.

The next morning as Dad was getting ready to go to work, April joined him at the table. "So, April, what do you think about Hugh?"

"Oh, Dad. Please don't." April said. "Hugh is a nice guy with a son. I am not interested."

"All I am saying is for you to think about it. He has repented, come back full status in the church and is busting his you know what to keep his career and raise his son. Not many guys would do that, he has changed. He is the Hugh we knew before," Dad said.

"Then you date him," April blurted out laughing. Dad did not say anything more, not to her anyway. He spent time conversing with the Lord asking Him to have a plan and knock these two heads together. They were best friends at one time and if you have that in a marriage, you will make it.

The days flew by, and thankfully she did not see Hugh. Elaine stopped by to drop some things off for her Mom, but April was playing the piano and did not stop. Miranda came into where she was playing and tapped her on the shoulder. April looked up and asked, "What did she have to say?"

"Honey, Elaine and I want to know if you would go to dinner at the Country Club just once before you go. You always liked it there."

"Okay," April said and kept playing. She felt she had to leave soon, or they would have her walking down the aisle with Hugh without her realizing it. They did not fully comprehend that she wanted a life of her own. As much as she loved them all, they all had expectations for her.

The Country Club was one of April's favorite places to go out to eat, not because it was ritzy, but because what they had inside was interesting and she loved that! There were old-fashioned dolls on display, some dressed in century clothing, complete with a parasol. Then there were pictures made out of wood, with displays of a barn raising, or wagons bringing in loads of hay or pioneer wagons, so detailed and real looking. The food was good, but the atmosphere was amazing.

During the dinner, April asked to be excused to go to the bathroom. When she came out Hugh was there waiting for her.

"May I talk to you for a few minutes?" He asked her. April was uneasy but she knew her mind and trusted her gut feeling. Hugh exited the building, and they stood outside on the wooden veranda.

"April, I know you are upset with me. I can't tell you how sorry I am for what has happened, but that is all behind me now. We all make mistakes, and I wish you would forgive me," Hugh said.

April looked at him and said, "I forgive you, Hugh. The truth is, I don't care anymore. I was in four different places that year, and twice I was offered marriage, but I did not love them. My heart belonged to you, and you smashed my feelings so bluntly. And yes, that made me angry. I never cheated on you, and I did have the opportunity."

Hugh looked frustrated. "I was weak, but what happened was a mistake with Sandy. I saw that shortly after we were on base. I can't take back what happened or what I did. I can only go forward, and I wish you would forgive me. I still care about you a lot., I am afraid you will discard my feelings out of your anger".

April replied, "I was angry with you, Hugh, but not anymore. Life is too short to be angry every day. I simply went on with my life."

Hugh looked at her directly. "For me nothing has changed. I want another chance with you. Will you please give me that? Just some time. That is all I am asking." he said.

April looked at him and said, "Time? My life belongs to the military, as does yours. I have no time to see anyone or have a relationship, but when I am discharged then my time is mine and I may or may not meet someone. I can't say what will happen," she honestly said.

"I just want you to wait for me. Give me that," Hugh said.

In her mind April thought, "I did that once before and it did not turn out," but there she was agreeing. She wanted to kick herself. She hated to hurt people's feelings, but all too often people walked all over her. And this would most likely be another one of those times. For the sake of trying, she stood there and agreed. Hugh kissed her cheek, and they went back into the Country Club and sat with their families.

Dad was all smiles, but everyone was eating and having conversations on their own. As the dinner progressed Dad tinged the side of his glass to make an announcement. "I am proposing a toast to the wellness of both April and Hugh, to be protected, safe, and come home." They raised their glasses and drank. April could feel Hugh's eyes on her, but she did not return his stare.

After dinner they gave hugs in the parking lot, then piled into their cars. The drive home was mostly silent. "So how did it go? Did Hugh speak to you?" Dad asked.

"Yes, he did, and he asked me to wait for him. And I said I would," she answered her Dad. And that was all that was said, nothing more.

The Ladies never judged her or made premature decisions. When she shipped out, she told the Ladies what her thoughts were. "I just want to meet someone who likes me for me, not hurt me," she brooded.

"You will someday, Dear. You will," they said as the sisters looked at each other. They knew in her heart she was hurt badly, and never wanted to go through that again. They did not blame her for avoiding Hugh and not wanting to be with or trust him again. It was time for both of them to move on, so they thought, but they kept their ideas to themselves. They knew better than to say what they thought to Miranda or Gordon. In time they felt April would work things out. She was a strong spirit.

As the days wound down, April realized, as did everyone else around her, she would be leaving soon. Miranda did arrange a big meal, a Christmas dinner the day before April left. There were twenty-two people in their home, including the Ladies, Judge Du Val and his lady, Miranda's parents, and some of the closest friends of theirs and April's. Obviously missing were the Marshalls. None of them were in attendance, and April was relieved.

There was a small gift exchange which was arranged long before the dinner. Each person was assigned one name to make a gift for. Yes, make! April had Manny's name. She whittled a tie tack for him, with a horse on the front. She had to go to the wielding shop to have the pin part adhered to the wood. That tie tack looked pretty amazing.

At the table each person took the gift from their lap or purse and put the wrapped gift on the table. There were no names on the gift so peaking did no good. After dinner, the head of the table began. Dad stood up and asked his gift to be passed to Lena.

Then it was Lena's turn. She stood and asked for her gift to be passed to Contessa, and so on. It was pretty amazing. All of the gifts were thoughtfully made, and everyone loved their gift. After that they all began to get up to say thanks and their goodbyes. Soon they all had left, and April helped to clean up. She loaded the dishwasher, while Dad put the leftovers in smaller containers. April saw that Miranda was tired, so she asked her Mom to sit down and boss them around while winking at her Dad.

As they sat in the living room the telephone rang. Her Dad handed April the phone. "Hello?"

"Hey, this is Diane. Do you still need that ride to the airport in the morning?"

"Oh. Yes, I do, and I appreciate you offering," April said.

"Okay. I will be there at 6 a.m.," and April hung up the phone.

"Who is taking you to the airport?" her Dad asked.

"Oh, Diane. You remember her. She was at the Christmas Community Center, and she is in the military as well. She goes back the same day I do, but she has wheels," April said.

"I would have gladly driven you," Dad said.

"I know you would, but she is going anyway, and you have your job. I hate being a burden to you," April said.

"April, you were never a burden to me, Darling. I love you. You do know that. Don't you?" her father asked her.

"Dad, I know you do, and I love you too. This is just easier on all of us."

"It's never easy," Dad said. "Just promise that you will try to be safe and come home to us, not in a box."

"I will try to do my best, Sir," she said as she stood and hugged her Father.

Back to Home Base and Another Mission

DIANE WAS THERE RIGHT AT 6 A.M. APRIL HAD ONE BAG. SHE HAD put Ruby in her room closing the door so she could not follow her.

Dad was up, but not downstairs yet. April opened the door, turning the knob so the door would lock when it was closed. It was dark, but she knew this sidewalk even with her eyes closed. She opened Diane's car door, hopped in, and asked if she could throw her bag in the backseat.

"Yeah, go ahead," Diane said.

They pulled out and Gordon watched from upstairs in the bathroom. The car lights left the driveway and onto the road. She was always leaving, and he shook his head. "God watch over her, because I cannot," he thought.

During the entire trip, Diane had the radio on and the two of them talked to catch up.

"So how did the date go with Hugh?" April asked.

"I called him, but he was busy. It was obvious he was not interested. He acted sort of snobbish if you know what I mean," she said.

April did not care. Sooner or later Hugh would bite. It was just a matter of time. A leopard does not change its spots, once a cheater always a cheater.

The ride was fast because Diane had a heavy foot on the gas pedal. At the airport Diane parked and they both hugged each other in full and different uniforms and went their separate ways.

In short order April found herself flying headed to her home base in Florida. This trip seemed so surreal. She tried to keep her feeling separate. It would be paramount for her to do so. So she suppressed them deep into her heart, nodded, said a prayer, and slept.

It was a nice flight, straight through without any interruptions. When she arrived at her home base, it was as if she had not left. Everything was the same. She checked her inbox for mail and sure enough there were a few letters. She mentally reminded herself to pick up some postcards off base.

There was also a formal letter from her company Commander. She tore open the envelope and noticed it was dated October 20th. As she read she was made aware there was another mission she was requested for, and to contact him as soon as possible.

April put the letter in her pocket and walked quickly to her Commander's headquarters. At the door she knocked, the door was opened, and a female secretary was at the desk who asked what she wanted. April pulled out the letter and was told to sit down and wait. The woman took April's letter with her and disappeared down a hallway. Soon she returned and asked April to follow her.

It sort of reminded April of high school, with more severe consequences than the principal's office. As they approached an end door, the secretary turned the door knob, stood back, and allowed April to enter.

As she stepped inside, there was her Commanding Officer with a five-star general sitting by a desk. April instantly saluted them and was told "at ease". They asked her to sit down. As the conversation ensued, they laid out the planned mission for her, should she decide to take it.

There were eleven men missing. They were listed as MIAs in Laos, but they may have been moved again to somewhere in Vietnam. This was their target. They were to be rescued, after being missing for thirty-five years.

April sat there thinking. She had light skin, blonde hair, light-colored eyes, and height wise she might pass. She did not know the language either, which presented a huge problem.

She brought up these concerns and was told they had everything in place should she decide to accept this mission. April asked what they had in mind.

"Well, we have a way to put an implant in your eyes to change them and a stitch or two to slant your eyes. We also have new technology that when you blink your right eye a window will appear, like on a computer screen, identifying what you are seeing. For example, a plant, if it is eatable or poisonous, or the identity of the man you are looking at. There is, of course, a corresponding implant in your head, which is connected to that eye. It is minimally invasive, and on prototypes worked well. Your skin can easily be tanned, and your hair color changed. This mission's window is two weeks. And after you return home with the MIAs, it can all be reversed with little recovery time."

April was intrigued. She was interested. "All I ask is you give me a few minutes to step out to make my decision," she said.

Her company Commander knew well of April's decision process. He knew she wanted to say a prayer before making any decision. "Permission granted. Don't take too long now, ya hear. There is a room across the hall," he said to her.

April left that room and opened the door across the hall. It was empty and very dark. She walked to a chair and knelt down.

She asked her Father in Heaven to guide her in this decision. She needed an affirmation of why and as she prayed, she got an extremely strong impression of her Dad and Judge Deval. Why that image she did not know, but these two people she trusted with her life. And she thought perhaps she was needed for the MIAs lives. She finished her prayer, got up, and went back to the room.

She again saluted the officers and sat down, "I would like to have more detail on this mission and with your approval I accept."

The officers smiled at each other. They were indeed pleased. They knew this soldier was quiet, resourceful, competent, dependable, honest, and for some reason seemed to have additional help when she needed it. In the missions she had in the past, many were accomplished without one single shot being fired.

They told her to take the file and read it from one end to the other. She was to make herself familiar with the maps, the terrain, any indigenous plants, the officers in charge on their last report, and where the men were believed to be held. They also told her arrangements would be made for her within the week for the surgery.

April left with the file in a thin notebook they had provided. As she passed the secretary, the woman called to her, "Good luck, and may God speed you all home." April nodded and left.

On her bunk she laid out the maps. Somehow this was familiar. It was crazy to think that, but it was. It truly was.

She had been in these woods before. The path to the village was familiar, in her dreams she had seen it all before. She also knew some faces in the village. Now it was a dream, but she trusted them. In the past, many things had been revealed that way.

Four days later April was in surgery. The surgeons put the implants in her eyes, and also implanted a devise in her head behind her right ear. And indeed when she blinked twice and looked at an object, it told her what it was and what it was used for.

They also put a device in her voice box. From this time forward when she would speak, the language of the village would come out. In order to speak English, she would have to hold her finger against her throat, apply pressure, and her English language would be heard. This was amazing technology, and she hoped she would not become confused and make a mistake.

Her hair was dyed, her skin darkened, and the stitches at her eyes were removed. She indeed looked more Asian then American. One last measure they sewed shut her private parts. She was to appear as a Down Syndrome person who roamed the forests, having been left by her Mother. She appeared abnormal to them, for her own safety.

She finished the advance weapon training three days ago with swords, knives, and hand to hand combat. She could handle any weapon and felt confident. As she came out of the hospital, she felt fine, but got many stares. No one knew who she was.

She reported to her company Commander, and even he looked at her oddly and hesitated.

She had to hold her hand against her throat to have him understand. His face flushed red. He welcomed her in and kept staring at her. "Well, I have to say, you have it all. If this does not work, I don't know what will. I am giving you one device that is crucial to this mission. It is a call device. When you press this button, choppers will be landing in the safest closest spot they can, within twenty minutes to a half hour away. So it is YOUR responsibility to make sure you are clear, far enough away from hostiles, and in the right place with all of the survivors. There will be a small canister in your pack to put down some red smoke. It will be enough for them to see your mark. Good luck. I wish you the best. Bring our boys back, and God speed you all home."

April walked out and went to her bunk to pack. When she saw Sergeant Bob, he came over to her and shook her hand. Then he pulled her to him and hugged her. "I believed you to be one of the best recruits I have ever trained. Now you go and show the others I was right," and he winked at her.

She was alone on this mission. She had no back up, no one to call for help. She had to rely on her gut instincts, her training, and prayer.

Packed and ready to ship out. She studied those maps again. She quickly realized as she blinked twice even the faces of men were identified, their names, and crimes committed. This was no vacation by any means. The men were ruthless. She felt an urge to pray. As she did, she felt the sweet companion of the Holy Ghost. Once again confirming to her that this mission was right. She was where she should be. April hated waiting, but she had to wait for her ride.

At 06:00 a.m. the chopper arrived. There were two pilots and two gunners. April handed her orders to the one while a gunner reached for her small bag. They were taken aback by her looks, but all of her paperwork was in order, and they soon were off the ground heading to Southeast Asia. This was going to be a long trip, so April found a place to rest and catch some Zs. She kept those maps near her at all times. Looking at the ones that seemed so familiar, she felt soon she would know why.

The trip took three days, from one chopper to another. At each new ride she was briefed. "This should hopefully be the last ride in," she said to herself.

The terrain was hilly and full of trees, plants, and shrubbery. She had a brief meal of rice and water. She wanted to keep it light and subsist on what she found to eat and scant rice. She felt optimistic there would be time to make a meal. She was counting on that.

As they flew into the drop point. They dare not enter the country, so she was dropped on the boarder and would have to hike through back country sixty or so miles to where she would find the men. April liked hiking with a machete in her hand. She was confident.

She walked and occasionally cut her way until dusk, then she saw a good-sized tree that looked snake free. She threw a rope and climbed up. She secured herself by tying her waist to the tree. She sat and listened to the sounds of the jungle. There were screeching monkeys, birds cackling, loons crying out, and frogs talking to each other in the water. It was soothing to April. As she relaxed listening to those sounds, she began to be sleepy.

All at once she awoke to the sound of screaming. It sounded human. She froze.

She did not want to sit there, but she was not sure what it was and did not want to reveal herself just yet. Then she heard the native talk of this island. Some men had speared a wild boar and were planning on how to get him back to camp. April listened, and she understood what they were saying. She could not see her hand in front of her face, but she knew they were very close.

She was not able to sleep soundly after that skirmish, but she was in and out of sleep. When dawn broke the air was foggy, cloudy, and thick. April heard a licking sound, and, as the clouds moved, she saw a wild animal eating the remains of the wild boar that the men had butchered. It was right at the base of the tree she was in. She untied the rope securing her to the tree and began her decent. On the ground the animals backed away. She followed the blood trail the men made while dragging the boar.

April stopped a good distance away from the camp. She made her way to a hillside with good ground cover. Below her was a stream of good water and water cress she could eat. She saw the boar hanging up by its back legs and suspended between two trees. This was as good a time as any to acquaint herself with the camp. So she began to sing a song as she walked along the creek. Instantly one of the guards heard her and investigated.

The guard brought April to the camp to the Captain for inspection. He looked at her curiously. He spoke to her harshly. "Where are you from?" he demanded.

April smiled at him like a child. Her eyes a bit crossed and she began to sing.

The Captain guessed right away that this was the mongoloid child that had been lost or abandoned about ten years ago. He stood and grabbed April's two arms in his strong hands and shook her.

"Please. Please, momma. I will be good," she said closing her eyes, and holding her head down.

Yes, he had found this ghost of a girl. How she had survived in the jungle was amazing. There had been sightings of her from other camps over the years. If she was hungry, she wandered into camp, and then mysteriously left again.

The Captain did not pursue questioning the dummy any further. He dismissed her and the girl wandered to the boar pig and then around the camp. She finally sat at a firepit and began making a sound as if she were hungry and putting her finger in her mouth.

The Captain called for some of the men to begin butchering the hog and make dinner for the camp. He had not had meat for quite some time, and the hog was young and should be tender. There was plenty for everyone, including the dummy.

April kept quiet, only singing lullabies, and rocking back and forth. Some of the men looked at her in disgust, thinking it was a shame she had been born. Some argued she survived on her own in a wild jungle with no help. She was not of value or of concern. They all felt she would disappear as she had in other encampments over the years.

Soon they were all eating. April was watching out of the corner of her crossed eye the man who left with meat in a bucket and bread in a basket. She got up to follow him and took the basket from him, walking. She knew he was most likely going to feed the captives and she needed to know where they were.

Within a six-minute walk they arrived at the bamboo jails the men were held in. Some were old, with grey hair and beards. Some were in bad health, weak, and breathing hard. Some stared at the wall. The guard pushed the bucket in the jail, and one man took it and divided the meat to all of the men. Then the basket April held was dumped on the floor, and the man picked up the bread blowing off the debris. The bamboo door was locked, and April stared at the men. She had counted eleven of them, and wondered if they would be strong enough to make the journey.

As they continued on, there was another jail holding nine more men. These men were in a jail partially underground in a cave with bamboo and metal surrounding them. These men looked in much better health. They were stronger and capable, which explained why there were two armed guards to watch them. They too were fed pork and bread. They ate it hungrily like dogs. April winced inside, she had never at any time known about a prisoner who was treated this disrespectfully. Soon she and the guard were heading back to camp. April swung the basket singing another childish song happily.

The guard shook his head as he watched her. She had a happy heart even after all she had been through. She had been abandoned, left to die, but she survived. Well at least no one would have to watch her, or care for her.

Back at camp April walked to the cabin of the Captain, yawned sleepily, curled up like a cat by his door, and slept. The Captain got a kick out of the brainless child. She had not the sense to know how to sleep on a bed. That night, however, one of the men decided it had been a long time since he had lain with a woman, and he tried to take April to his bed. She screamed, gouged his eyes, bit him, slapped him over and over, and kicked him between his legs. She fought like an animal. And as angry as the Captain was at the man, he laughed at her. She was like his puppy.

In the morning April took it upon herself to feed the men in the jails. The guard gladly handed her the basket of bread, vegetables, and potatoes. She skipped with the baskets to the first jail. She knocked as was the custom. As the man inside came for the basket, April put her hand on her throat and said, "Do not look at me. Keep your eyes to the floor. I am from the US here to rescue you all and take you home," and the man looked up. April hissed at him. "Eat all that I bring, all of it. You must become stronger. Walk, exercise, and do all you can to become fit to walk this jungle. Do you understand?"

The man quietly said, "Yes." He took the bread and vegetables, and April left.

The second jail was much the same, but the man there kept staring at her. "Don't look at me," she said quietly.

The man knew and as he took the basket items to the cave, he told his men. They felt a sense of relief but had to contain themselves. The man then came back with the basket throwing it at her and screaming, "You idiot, retard," and April was glad. It was good that the guards think that the men hated her.

Back at camp April resumed her same sleeping post and slept peacefully. In the morning she was cooking breakfast of pancakes made from corn she had gathered and berries to put on top. The Captain was impressed. She had enough for everyone in camp. This gave her the right to go where ever she wanted to collect berries and whatever else she wanted to cook.

April took that opportunity to take more food to the men in the jails. She took them nuts, berries, cooked yellow potatoes, bananas, and beans with rice. Meat was in every dinner. It was in pieces, so everyone got meat, not just the guards. Everyone ate better.

By the time a week was up, April felt it would soon be time to make their move. She knew that the men were all feeling better in the first jail. The realization that they would have a chance to escape and possibly go home was foremost in their minds. They knew to say nothing, not even to each other.

That afternoon another group of men came into camp, bringing with them more prisoners. The men had their arms tied to a ladder. As they walked, it was obvious they were all stiff and weak. Most likely they had walked like that all day.

There were five more prisoners, so that was twenty five in all, twenty six with her. And depending on the chopper there would be one or two pilots, that is twenty eight. There are two gunners, makes thirty. She hoped the chopper could get them all out, but nevertheless she was concerned. So much so that one evening April had taken some foil with her and made a calling signal. She had some materials with her, wire and what she needed to use to get a message to her home base.

The clerk at the base was confused when the message was received. It read: *Found 26 STOP hope to bring them all out STOP may need 2 choppers STOP will be in touch in more days on Evac STOP.* The clerk took the message to his Commander. Then he took it to the top brass who sat at his desk and smiled.

She had made it; she had found them. He would be sure to send in what she needed to bring all of them home. He picked up his phone dialing a code. He explained the situation and was assured two choppers would deploy from the Southeast Asian site within twenty minutes of her sending that signal. They would send out pilots and choppers now, to see that everything would be in place when that signal came in.

April calculated in her mind what to do and when. She had already informed the new men who were tied out like dogs on stakes. They were strong, had not been held long, and were willing to die to get out.

April searched for a poisonous berry that was in this area. One that did not kill, but rendered an animal helpless, like one used when hunting with darts. That berry would paralyze victims for seven to eight hours. That would be just enough time for her to help all of the prisoners escape and make it to the pickup sight.

She picked a huge basket of the berries that had the sweetest taste and a purple color. At 3 a.m. she smashed the berries and cooked them. She made pancakes, with blueberry-syrup. At 6 am the cook was there, wanting a taste. April slapped his hand, and he laughed at her.

By 8:00 a.m. the heat swelled, and everyone had been fed. Within an hour most were sleepy. This was her time to move. April made it to the first jail. There the guard was out cold. She loosened the peg and took the guards gun with her. The men filed out one at a time. Two had trouble walking. They were stiff from being held captive for so long without exercise. The men in the yard were cut free, and they helped the men who were struggling to keep up.

At the underground jail, April opened the door, and the men came to her all smiles. Not one word was said. They all followed one another up the hillside path. The guard dog was barking constantly. April knew she had to put the dog down, he had been trained to track. With great regret she coaxed the dog to her in a happy voice, held him tightly telling the dog what a good boy he was, and as he relaxed in her arms with his tail wagging, she turned his head quickly and snapped his neck. It was over in seconds. She felt that he felt the only love and compassion was in the end of his life. She hurried to catch up with the men.

They were near the top of the hill when April whistled like a bird and one saw her, she motioned for them to get off the path and go right, through the scrubs down into the thick of the jungle. April knew then why this seemed so familiar. This was the path she had dreamed about so many times. She was out in front of the men and as her dream had shown her where snake pits were, where boar dens were, she was able to avoid each pit of danger, they kept moving.

April knew the men were tired, but they had to keep going. She had gathered some leaves which held residual moisture earlier and had them in the basket she carried. She gave them to the men who folded them to produce some water droplets which they drank eagerly.

She held her hand to her throat, "We must keep going. We need to be a good halfway to three-quarters of the way to our pickup site. We need to help each other, and I will find food along the way."

The men watched her. She knew each berry, mushroom, and stalk that was edible. She picked or cut them and handed them to the men. By nightfall it was obvious the men had to rest, however, it would be about now that the guards would be awake. They would have great headaches, but that would not stop them. They would pursue them. She told them one hour was all they would have to rest. They had to push on.

April was right. As the men awoke about 4:00 p.m. that evening, all of them either had headaches or vomited constantly leaving them weak. They drank water to flush their bodies of the toxin. They were not aware what had happened until almost 6 p.m. when they discovered the prisons were empty. "How did this happen? Who would have done this?" The dummy was not in sight, but surely, she did not do this. The cook wiped his finger in the residue of a plate that had the blueberry syrup. He tasted it and began to look around. It took him quite a while, but he found the site where the cooked berries had been buried. He got the Captain immediately. They had been fooled. "This could not have been the dummy who had been left to die. This was an imposter. Find her. Find them." The entire encampment of men, some not 100%, were scouting and walking to find their prisoners and the girl who tricked them.

Meanwhile the hour had been up. Some of the men who were weak were carried by the strong. They took turns carrying the three weakest men. At last April saw the boarder. It was barely daylight about 8 p.m. She pressed the button signal and knew within twenty minutes they would all be out of there.

The village guards were angry and determined to bring their prisoners and the culprit back. They were doing double time on their run. They were strong men with a strong work ethic. They would find them and bring them back.

April and her group of men sat down at the border. Some of the men were crying, and some were thanking her, but she said nothing. It was not over yet.

She heard the choppers. They were coming in fast. She popped some red smoke, and the pilots saw the red smoke immediately as they came to land. It all happened as fast as they landed. They came under fire. April turned her head and saw some of the village guards running toward them shooting.

"Well, it's them or us," she said to herself, and she began to shoot, one, two, three. As the choppers landed, a gunner gave her some assistance, seven, eight, nine. Then she backed toward the chopper as she kept shooting. Never were there more than four at one time. All of the men were on board now, and as she stepped on the chopper running board, she felt a sharp piercing of pain at her leg. She had been hit. She half turned and cut that shooter down, but there were more. She rolled onto the chopper as they began to lift off. She felt pain in her shoulder and grabbed for a gunner's saw gun and began to pelt bullets.

As they flew out, April realized one of the pilots had been hit too, in the chest area. She asked for someone to drag him into the area where they were. One of the newest prisoners had been a pilot and was able to assist to get them back safe. As they carried the man in, April took his jacket off and stripped him down. She never looked at his face, until she was about to make an incision to take the bullet out, then she saw it was Hugh.

She was taken aback, shocked. She tried to compose herself, but the others knew something was wrong. She was professional. She felt where the bullet entered. She turned the Hugh's body over and did not see an exit wound. She knew the bullet was still in his body. April guided her hand along his back and felt a protruding hard spot and knew that was it.

"I need some help," she said. "Someone hold him steady," and she checked in his flap which told his blood type. "Who here has Type AB blood. I may need some blood so whoever has that, rollup your sleeve." Two of the men responded. April burned the thin knife she had and made a half inch incision in his back. The bullet plopped out, the blood was contained, and in five minutes April was sewing up the incision. The bullet had penetrated his side, just missing his lungs.

April was spent, burned out emotionally, and she had forgotten she had been hit too. She wiped that same knife in alcohol, reburned it until the metal was black, and wiped the blade. Then she bent her leg, gritted her teeth, and made the incision. She threw her head back when some of the men steadied her. One took the knife and with a few flicks, the bullet fell on the floor. Then on to the shoulder area. It was clear that the bullet had exited and had missed bone. April was pulled back to the side wall of the chopper. She and Hugh lay there together throughout the flight to safety.

April was in and out of sleep. She thought, as she opened her eyes, from time to time she saw people walking around, and Hugh talking to her, but she could not distinguish if it was real or a dream.

When they landed, she, Hugh, and four others were taken for medical attention.

Most of the men were not injured, but they were emancipated and weak. April lay in the hospital bed. She felt grief that this mission was not as successful as the last. She knew she had taken lives and she cried. She understood that it was either them or her unit and she knew what she did, she had to do. Her biggest guilt was the dog. He was intelligent and strong, and she had to cut his life short so they would be safe. Accepting that was difficult.

Soon some of the men came to visit her. They wanted to thank her and know more about her. April explained most of what they saw was not her. She was from California, had blonde hair and fair skin. One of the captives was from California and asked what her name was.

"Di Angelo," April said.

The soldier was excited and asked if she was related to Gordon Di Angelo.

"Yes," April said. "Gordon Di Angelo is my Dad," and the man began to weep.

"He was my partner. Gordon and I ran missions until one night when I was taken captive."

Another asked, "What was Gordon's other friend's name?"

They thought and April said, "Is it Du Val?"

Their eyes lit up and one said, "Du Val saved my butt. He put down a fire wall that got us out of a jam." They talked for quite a while. As April listened, she knew why she was sent on this mission. It all became clear to her now and with this realization, she began to cry. How great God is to have found use for her, to let her know she was needed, AND to help her on the way keeping her safe to bring them all back home.

Soon she was boarding a chopper to bring her stateside. She had not healed yet, but felt that once the surgeries were reversed, she would be all right.

And she was. Within a week April was out and about on the grounds of the base. She sat on a bench to watch the waves roll in. It was so relaxing and peaceful. The breeze was warm and welcoming, then someone came and sat down beside her. It was Hugh.

"You're a difficult person to find," he said to her. "I did not know how to describe you, either as a Southeast Asian looking person or how I last remembered you". April sat there saying nothing, only smiling; she prayed he could not hear her mind racing. "I want to thank you," Hugh said, as he touched her arm. "I never saw the incoming, I did not know, and I don't believe there was anyone on board who would have known what to do but you."

"Hugh, the bullet was not life threatening. I only wanted to make sure it was out. I did not know the extent of the injury and did not want infection to set in," April told him.

"Well, I wanted to thank you," Hugh said as he stared at her. Then he began to get up to leave.

April was confused. When she realized who he was on that chopper, it bothered her. Was it hate or what was it something else? She did not know. As Hugh was leaving, April called out to him, "Good Luck. See you back home sometime."

Hugh turned to wave so she would see him.

While April walked in the other direction, she had to admit she felt indifferent with Hugh. Or did she? Maybe it was just her trying to save someone injured and she was surprised it was Hugh. For over two years she doubted she had any feeling for him anymore. No one likes their feelings being hurt, but there was no denying she felt something.

Eight days later April was back at her home base in Florida. She had some slight pain in her leg, but nothing that slowed her down. Sergeant Bob found her in the mess hall very early one morning when she could not sleep. He sat down and they talked.

He told her that she had done good. This mission was so crucial to the US, since many soldiers were still missing in other countries, and these men deserved to come home. April told Sergeant Bob the connection to her father, and she wanted to let her Dad know. "By all means, do it," Sergeant Bob told her. "These men will need all the help they can get to resettle back in civilian life."

"There is something else I need to talk about to you," Sergeant Bob said. "There is a lot of bad blood between you and the kickbox trainer, Paul. I don't know why, but sooner or later he is going to challenge you to the cage. And I for one don't want you to get beaten and hurt. So some of the guys and I want to work with you, so you are ready."

April looked at him incredulously, "Are you kidding me?" she asked.

"No, I am not. As juvenile and stupid as this is, none of us like it. This is one person perpetrating this stupid act. One! And we would like to see him gone. If you can beat him at his own stupid game, then he would be out!"

April knew that each time she saw trainer Paul there were ugly comments. He would often shove her, trip her, or try to make her look bad for no reason. If he did not like you, your life would be hell. "Okay, when and where?" she asked.

Sergeant Bob leaned back taking his cigar out of his mouth and laughed. "We can't let this get out. I will have someone get a message to you. We will begin your training within a day or two, but it is not happening, understand?" he said.

April realized all of them would be in trouble. She would have to train without being seen. No one could say anything or else.

She left Sergeant Bob and headed out to call her Dad. She was not sure what day it was, or what time it was in California. So she politely stopped another female officer and asked her. That officer knew of April's mission, and it was understandable to be confused what day or time it was after all she had been through.

April dialed the number from memory. It was early, 6 a.m. there.

The phone rang. "Hello," her Dad said.

"Hi, Dad. It's me, April. Do you have a minute?"

"Oh, sure, sure I do, Sweetie. What's on your mind?" he asked her.

"Dad, are you sitting down?"

He replied, "No, but I can. Is the news that bad?"

"No. Fact is, the news is that good," she said. "Do you remember Hal, Kyle, and Ben from your service days?"

"Oh, yes. Yes, I do. Sadly Hal was captured long ago. I lost contact and did not know of his whereabouts or even if he made it back," he said to her.

"Well, he did," April said. "That was my last mission. Twenty-six of them came back," she said. Her Dad was silent. April swore she could hear him weeping. "Dad, Dad, are you there?" she asked.

"I am here," and for sure her father was crying. "Dad, I am so sorry, I didn't mean . . ."

"No, don't say that, April," with deep breaths. "It is good to know. I mean, we were like brothers. Was there any word from John? He was sort of a big fellow with red hair. He was Du Val's partner."

April just said, "Yes. Dad, it was amazing. I was to bring back eleven and there were twenty-six in all. God knew and he used me as his instrument."

Her Dad was still crying. "I need to tell . . ." he said then blew his nose. Well, maybe we can come down there, just the two of us. I will talk to him today. This is great news, really it is. My heart is singing, and I know his will be too. I can't thank you enough. These men were family to us, and we thought they were lost."

April told her Dad the men were in another place, not where she was. And indeed, it would be awesome if they both could come, speak to the men, and help them to resettle into civilian life.

Inside of her she wanted to remind him of how both of them had protested her wanting to go into the military, but she couldn't. She knew loss, and it would be like adding salt to a wound. She could not do that to her Dad.

"Okay, Dad. I am going to hang up now. Give Mom a hug from me. Okay?"

"I will, Sweetie, and thanks for calling," and the call ended.

"Miranda, Miranda!" Gordon screamed. Miranda came running down the stairs.

"What's wrong, Gordon? Are you all right?" Gordon Di Angelo's face was wet with tears, and he was smiling from ear to ear.

Miranda was perplexed when Gordon told her. She too began to cry tears of joy. "I will call and see if I can get a flight for the four of us," she said.

"No, don't. Let me tell my friend Du Val first, and we will go from there."

Gordon Di Angelo drove to work happier than he had been in a long, long time. He had felt it was a mistake for his daughter to go into the military, but now, just look what God had led her to. He shook his head, "Amazing. Simply amazing," he said.

He entered his office and the first thing he did was to call his lifelong friend. "Hey, listen. It's me, Gordon, and before you razzle me, I have something crucial to tell you." When he finished, the two men were crying together on the telephone.

There were many questions that Gordon could not answer, and he suggested they all fly down together to meet their old friends after they were debriefed and ready.

"I'm in," Du Val said. "It will be great."

They mutually hung-up feeling like they did a great thing. Both of them were humbled to their knees and thanked God for the return of these men to the US. And they were thankful that they might be returned to their families. They prayed that they would be healed. They hoped that they would be able to help these men, and that their hearts would be willing. Then they thanked God for having a part in April's life that might not have been. And that she stood strong in her convictions to enter the military. Had she not, those men still would be there. They thanked their Father in Heaven for all his kind, merciful blessings, those seen and unseen. Indeed, they all had much to be thankful for.

April began her training with Sergeant Bob and several other men who were proficient in kickboxing, judo, and jujitsu. These men were skilled and hard driven and had April practice over and over and over. Her body would become sore, and black and blue, but she was determined not to give up. Her training was sometimes as early as 3 a.m. or late as 11 p.m., sometimes it was an hour at lunchtime. Whenever they practiced, it was just one on one, and no one knew.

For weeks, sometimes three times a day, April worked hard, harder than she ever had. It was just like frogman training. In several of the last of her sessions, April was able to best her teacher. He would get up and smile at her while shaking her hand.

Within days after her many months of training ended, the opportunity presented itself. Trainer Paul came from behind her, slapping April in her back, pushing her forward so hard she went down in the dirt. She got up spitting dirt and spit into Paul's face. He felt insulted and challenged her to the mat. On the mat were a group of new trainees who had just enlisted. They all cleared the ring, scattering like mice.

"I am going to break your face, you disgusting witch!" Paul screamed at April.

She was not afraid. As she stepped into the ring, she saw six of her trainers, including Sergeant Bob. "Are you inviting judges or is this whatever goes?" April asked him.

"What? You're afraid?" he taunted her.

"No. I am not afraid, but when I beat you fair and square. I want witnesses, so your butt is out of the honorable service of the US. You are not an honorable man. You are nothing but a bully," she seethed at him.

He lunged at her.

April stepped nimbly aside. The four corners had spotters, two she knew, and two she did not. She did see Sergeant Bob nod his head and remove his cigar.

"WHATEVER!" Paul screamed rushing at her, springing in the air, and trying to hit her with his feet. Make no mistake, this man was a professional, but an arrogant professional. He did make mistakes, minor ones, but that is when April struck. It took twenty-two minutes for Paul to be lying in his own blood with a broken leg, fractured ribs and collar bone, with black swollen eyes, and half crying.

April was not free of injury. Her arms were sore, and he had gotten in some good shots at her backside. But it was over. She was tired and weak from the exhilaration of the fight.

The marshals came with cuffs. They had to lift Paul and carry him out. That was the last time Paul would bully her, or anyone else never again.

As April limped out, two of her trainers assisted her. Sergeant Bob bumped one out of the way. He was proud to escort this tiger. She was his best recruit, and he was proud of that!

April was not excused from regular duty. That fight did not happen in the eyes of her Commander. They were all glad Paul was gone. He did not represent the US with honor, but nevertheless this soldier was not privileged. She was expected to exercise, participate in group events, and April pushed through the pain. Every night she let the hot water soak those sore spots. Days later her body was black and blue. By day ten her body was yellow in many spots, but she was feeling stronger every day. The workouts and runs were a welcomed distraction. She did all she could to stay in shape. The more she pushed her body, the better and stronger she felt.

It had been months since her last mission and April's two year mark was up in six months. She wondered if she would be deployed again. There was no war that the US was involved in. So, more than likely, when her two year and some odd months were up, she would be going home.

Home sounded sort of odd. These men and women had been her home. But her family was at home. They are the ones she loved most. Nope, no re-enlistment for her. She had a life to live and wanted it.

Gordon Di Angelo and Du Val were true to their word. The two couples did fly down to Florida and met their comrades. It was tearful and soul searching. Several of them no longer had families. Some of their parents had passed away, and they wanted to go to their gravesites. Some had been married, and out of those who were married only two women waited all that time. The others had moved on to another life alone or with another husband. It was difficult for all of them in one way or another.

Gordon did offer them jobs if they decided to come to Fresno, and of course Mr. Stevens was more than helpful in finding jobs for others. The men who chose to work on the D Farms loved their jobs. They loved the freedom, the solitude, and the wide-open spaces. There were people to talk to or not. It was their choice. They were treated well by everyone in town and the local chapter of the veterans' organization was available.

Another Mission

APRIL HAD BEEN DILIGENT THIS PAST YEAR IN SENDING POSTCARDS, and it was weekly she found mail in her box. So much that she had trouble keeping up with it all. Of course she loved getting mail, but sometimes it just was more than she could respond to.

One envelope looked different than the rest. She tore open the card and low and behold the judge was getting married in December and this was her invitation. "Well, what do you know?" she said out loud. She was happy there was nothing better she could have wished for her sort of uncle and friend. Finally!

She had time off here and there and was able to find a lovely silverware set. It was quite expensive though and her salary was not much. She passed it over and kept looking.

It was days later when she found the perfect gift for them. It was a Persian rug in a shop, and it was for sale. It was reasonable, like brand new, and the fibers and designs were lovely, not loud.

April knew the Judge's home had a huge front room and this would look very nice in there. The room had cherry walls, and this rug was light yellow and white with flecks of red and it would be perfect. The cost was sixty four dollars to ship it to them, so in all it was cheap. As she was paying for the shipment, her cell phone rang. It was her Commanding Officer.

"Hello, Sir," she said.

"D, we need you back here as soon as you can get here. We have a job for you."

She hung up walking to her vehicle saying, "Ding dang it anyway," and scuffing the toe of her boot in the dirt.

As she parked and headed to her Commander, she was handed a file. It was another retrieve mission.

"So how much do you like swimming?" he asked her.

"Well. I do like swimming a lot, but in clean water, no sharks, jelly fish, or poisonous things," she said.

Her Commander laughed and then said, "Well, I know you like four legged animals of all sorts. That is how your name came to mind for this mission," he said.

April sighed, "How long is this one? What is my time frame?"

"Four days, in and out and you will be on your own."

"Wow," she thought to herself. As always she asked to be excused to say a prayer and she returned smiling.

The mission was simple retrieve a criminal from a foreign country. He would be on a ship in the middle of the ocean. That was frightening to her.

April was confused. How she would swim from the middle of the ocean and how would she get this guy off of the ship willingly? He was much bigger than she was, and a criminal, so throwing him off the ship was not an option.

"I see smoke coming out of those ears," her Commander laughed at her. "All you need to do is make contact, restrict him, and get him off of that steamer. We will do the rest."

She agreed.

April was boarding a plane within two days. Her only backup was another female officer she had not yet met. As they touched down in Morocco, their contact provided them with a change of clothing so they would fit in and had arranged for them to escort a herd of goats onto the ship bound for Persia. The two women officers fit in. The goats were not tame, but not out of control. As they walked through the village to where the ship was boarding, the goats followed them like dogs.

Once they boarded, the only area to keep the goats was topside on the ship. They had made contact for transport late. The deck men made a makeshift area to keep the goats inside. To be content with minimal hay and water collected in barrels. April set about to secure grain for the goats. She knew if they were full they would be quiet. That same day, the ship set sail. The women in their peasant garb were quiet and kept to themselves and the goats.

By nightfall some of the deckhand guards were mulling around topside and pushed April by gun point to the side. They told her to stand still as they frisked her for weapons. They did the same to her companion. No weapons were found, but she felt exposed.

There seemed to be a disagreement, an argument of sorts. Money amounts were being mentioned and soon April was pushed by gun point to the interior of the ship. Her companion was not allowed to follow. From bits and pieces she learned she had just been sold as a concubine.

"Dang, just my luck," she said to herself. They took her to a door and knocked with their rifles.

"Enter," someone said.

Inside, the room was lavishly decorated with silk trailed down from the ceiling to the floor with several chandeliers. There was lush carpeting on the floor, beautiful furniture, and fine furnishings all around. The man on the bed was the man she was to bring back. He was barely recognizable, no longer was tall and in sleek conditioning as in the photo. He was fat. So fat that April

161

knew she would have to drug him to get him out. She groaned inside but never showed that to them. The fat man ordered the guard out and beckoned April to him. She danced to beguile him. She turned and swirled in her colorful cloak, then she dropped the cloak and danced more all around the bedsides.

The man lunged for her, but April nimbly danced away from him. As she turned, she saw weapons in the room on the dresser tops. There were guns, whips, handcuffs, rope, and bottles of chloroform. Ah, yes. Those would come in handy. She danced over to where the handcuffs were and began using them as castanets clicking them together. As she danced, she approached her target. She pushed his hands down, stepped up onto his bed, and stood over him. The man was delighted, smiling, and laughing. She leaned forward letting her false long hair dangle into his face, and then she sat on his legs.

The man reached for her, and she took his one hand, kissed it, and placed a cuff on that wrist. The man was surprised but laughed. He was loving this game. April snapped that wrist to the bedpost directly behind the man's head. Then she reached for his other hand as he tried to grab at her. She nuzzled his cheek with her nose as she slid up his face. Then she attached the other cuff to his free hand and snapped it onto the other bedpost. With his hands secured, she then got a small rope and bound his feet together. She danced again over stepping him and went to the dresser that had the chloroform. She doused a large amount onto the bottom of her dress and quickly jumped up onto the bed, sitting on the man's chest as he smiled. She pulled up the dress covering his face.

The man suddenly realized this was not a seduction. He wriggled and tried to break her hold on his face. April held the cloth tightly over his face, nose, and mouth so he would inhale the drug. Within seconds he was out. She looked around. There was only one window available to her, and it was just a porthole. He would never fit through that. She had to think fast!

There was a knock on the door. April went to it pinching her face to look flushed. She barely cracked open the door telling the guard to send in another woman. She could not keep up. The guard laughed and soon returned with April's companion. The picking was easy, they were the only two young women on the ship.

As her companion entered the room, April lunged at the unsuspecting guard pulling him into the room by his rifle barrel. She pulled it from him as her companion knocked him to the ground with her feet. April used the stock of the gun to knock him in the head. He was out cold.

"I have him. He is out like a light. We can't get him through that small window. We have to get him overboard somehow," April said.

Her companion agreed. It was all they could do to lift, push, and pull that man to the outer corridor of that room in order to get him overboard.

April looked quickly at her companion. "I sure hope they send help. I do not relish swimming in this ocean."

With that the companion said, "I am right behind you." They both gave a mighty shove, and the man went over with April at his backside, and the companion followed.

As the boat passed them, the waves pushed them away and the three of them floated for what seemed like a long time. April knew it was crucial to keep the fat man on his back, so he did not suffocate in the water and drown. As they waited the water was pitch black, and the sky was pitch black. There was not a star in sight. It was so ominous and unknowing. Soon they felt waves coming from underneath them. Before they knew it, they were being lifted up by a metal platform. It was a submarine that had been submerged waiting for them. April was relieved. As they were on solid ground of the sub, men came out to assist them. They identified themselves and briefed the two women as others towed the man to a place inside the submarine.

Once inside the women were scurried to a cabin and given standard uniforms. They were deep navy-blue jumpsuits. April did not care. They were bulky but dry and warm. They put on caps that were given to them, turned the latch that was on the door, and walked out. They were greeted by a seaman who escorted them to a briefing room with their Captain.

The Captain was a much older man. April knew of him. She had seen his photo hanging in a hallway back in her camp. This man had years of sailing experience. She was relieved they were the ones to retrieve them.

As the two women sat there, the Captain wanted to know the details of the abduction of this notorious outlaw. April told the Captain how it all came about and how they got the man out of his cabin and overboard. The Captain looked at them.

April swore his eyes danced with a smile.

The Captain leaned back and said, "You ladies sure made this easy on us. Two captive concubines, they will assume he threw you overboard and you dragged him along. They will most likely conclude you all drowned since you are missing. Nice job. Very nice job. We will be stateside in about five days. Meanwhile make yourselves comfortable here on our ship."

April had no intention of exploring a ship full of men. That was risky. Men are men, and they were the only two women on board. Politely the female officers thanked the Captain. They said they would remain in their cabin, so long as there were books to read or paper to write on, they would be fine.

The Captain agreed that would be best.

Not only were there magazines, books, and paper, but they had a radio and could listen to music, talk, and hear news from around the world. They slept, watched the ocean from their tiny window, read, and wrote. And as repetitious as that was, they arrived in five days back in the states, as promised safe and sound. Once on solid ground, April thanked her companion telling her she was so glad she was along with her when she was initially told she would have no help. The woman acknowledged and said she knew she was going. She was just waiting for April to come back home to base.

Next Stop Iraq

Mind games, there were a lot in the military, but April was not afraid, not anymore. She was done with fear. She wanted to live, and she thought that one day she would look back on this time and know she made a difference in some ways to her country and to other's lives. She would know she had lived, not wished for it, but did it!

April was sitting on her bunk. She had just finished a fifteen-mile run when a young lieutenant came to her with a note, again. She was asked to come to her Commanding Officer, pronto. All sweaty with a dirt-streaked face, she walked briskly to the Commanding Officer's headquarters. She entered and saw the same woman at the desk the woman who pressed a button on an intercom. "D is here as you requested, Sir." With that the woman told April to go back. She knew the way.

April knocked at the door. "Enter," she heard and went in.

It had become a familiar routine, but as she sat there she was attentive as if it were her first time. "D, we have a situation in Iraq. It seems there are bunkers somewhere in that damn desert sand that hold information, weapons, and dangerous chemicals. We would like you to go and lead a group to search for and find these bunkers. There are mine fields and very few honest people because they are afraid. You will be provided horses and gear. You will have a month or less, and you will be working with US ground troops, giving information daily.

April sat there a bit dazed. She had no preparation for this mission. So, as usual, she got up and crossed the hallway. She opened the door, sought out a place to kneel, and prayed.

This time was not as clear as in the past. "I am not my own boss, Father. You are, I know. I make choices on my own, but I cannot and will not live without you in my life. I need you as much as I need the air that I breathe. I depend on the companion of the Holy Ghost. Without him, I am lost. So please, Father in Heaven, guide me. Help me do what is right." She waited a bit, then rose up to go back to the Commander.

April sat down slowly, hesitantly and looked at her Commander. "Sir, I have mixed emotions about this. I know you have the last word. You are my boss, so whatever you think is right, I will do," she said.

"Well, hell. I didn't call you here to play a game of pick and choose. Of course I want you to go," so that was it.

April took the packet of orders, saluted him, and left. This was not such a happy feeling mission at all. She dismissed the negativity and began to whistle as she walked.

She stuffed the packet inside her pillowcase and went to take a long hot shower. It was lunch time. She was going to forgo it, read the packet, and have a power bar. Clean and dressed she pulled out the packet and read. She would be leaving as soon as a team was in place. She was going to Iraq to search and find. She would be assigned to an equestrian unit upon her arrival. All the horses were military trained as well as their riders. She had her own training. So when was she leaving? Hum.

April decided to subject herself to hot conditioning. She ran with insulated and heavy clothing. She spent nights outside, sleeping only on a sheet, no matter how cool it got. Sergeant Bob admired her. He helped her where he could and if he did not know, he found the source for her. She prepared herself as best as she could every day.

Within weeks the Commander received a telegram informing him that the team had been assembled and they were waiting for his contact to arrive. Again April was out running, and the messenger had to wait for her and her troop to return. Again, grimy, sweaty, and tired April walked to the Commanding Officer's office. She received her orders, saluted him, and left to collect her things.

As she showered she began to feel an ominous force within her chest. She knew what that was. She dried off and making sure no one was in her area, knelt with her towel around her, her hair looking like a mop, and she prayed. "Father, I felt the power of the Holy Ghost deep within me and I ask the Father for thy help to understand. I am not afraid, Father. I am unknowing, uncertain. How I am to do what I have been asked. Father, help me to understand, help me to know. I am always willing to serve thee, Father. Help me to understand. I humbly pray. Amen."

She dressed and took her small bag with her. She knew there would be other clothing waiting for her when she arrived at the Iraqi base. There was a flight for 128 troops shipping out to Iraq. They all looked so young, most were eighteen or nineteen years old. As she boarded, they saluted her due to the insignia on her uniform. She said to each one, "At ease". She truly felt that she should be saluting them for their willingness and bravery to serve. The flight was too quiet on this long ride to Germany.

During the flight April loudly said, "Will each of you state where you are from, starting from where I am, and go in rows up one side and down the other, then repeat. The soldiers were from almost every state in the US, but one third were from Pennsylvania and stationed at Fort Hood or from upstate New York.

April stood up and announced, "Look I am not your Commanding Officer. In fact, I am no one. I don't exist. But if I could offer you something that would help you, that one thing would be for you to pray. No one has the right to take away your belief in God. This is your God-given right. Sometime sooner or later you will call out to him. So I encourage you to develop a relationship with him through prayer."

One soldier near her looked at her and he said, "Ma'am, I don't know how to pray." Some laughed at him.

April said, "It's not funny and not his fault if he was never taught. Prayer is easy, it is done in a sequence. 1. You ask your Father in Heaven to hear you. Or you come before him in the name of Jesus Christ, because no one reaches the Father except through his son Jesus Christ. 2. Then you thank him. 3. Then you ask him for what you want or need. There is a difference. 4. Then you close in the name of Jesus Christ, Amen."

That same soldier asked what 'Amen' means.

"Amen means, Yes, it is so, in agreement, you affirm what you said," April told him.

The soldier thanked her.

She saw that soldier had written the four steps down in his cuff. "I promise you, that he never fails. He will always answer you. Maybe not right away, but he will. Remember often his answer is to wait. Please do include him on things you wonder about such as your spouse, children, parents, grandparents, or your animals. Include prayer at all meal, morning, and night. If you do not develop a relationship and know him, how will he know you?" she said.

Then she sat down, and a female soldier asked her, "How do you know this to be true?"

April told her, "Because I have lived this way all my life and I know it works. I have put it to the test all my life. You need to listen without speaking or questioning. Learn to listen. He will let you know by the power of the light of Christ which is given to all upon their birth.

"Oh, wow. I didn't know that," she said. Everyone now seemed settled and calm. April hoped that what she offered helped. She had no intention of taking anything away from what they believed in. She only wanted to add to it and to give them hope.

Touch down in Germany and April could feel the tension. The soldiers' moods had changed. She grabbed the soldier closest to her and said, "Don't be afraid. Stay strong from inside. Don't fret before you need to, or you will be all over the place inside. At battle you need to be focused and calm."

He smiled at her and said he had been trained that way and thanked her for the reminder.

She told him to be sure to pass this on to all the others, not just a select few.

That is where they parted ways. They went on to another transport and April headed to a chopper that was waiting for her. She was heading to an outpost, not a base.

From Germany that flight was about two hours. It gave April a good chance to catch up on some sleep. Yes, sleep! She had learned to sleep when and where she could to keep her mind alert. She hated feeling overtired and groggy which often was part of a mission. So she slept when she could, even on a noisy chopper.

When she arrived at her destination, it was a remote outpost. The dust and sand flew about them making visibility almost zero. She put a cloth over her mouth and partially covering her eyes to keep the sand out.

As she walked to a cave-like tent area, a tall slim man walked towards her to welcome her.

"Welcome," he said with an Arabic sounding accent. His name was Sal. That was what he went by, no Captain, Sergeant, or Sir. Just Sal. He said his name was so difficult to pronounce that it was easier for the soldiers to say, "Sal."

April liked him immediately, and they sat in the cave to discuss what the mission entailed and any problems that might arise.

"It is well known that there are bunkers buried in the sand and hillsides that are undetectable by aircraft. It is necessary to go by foot to find them. However, there are also mine fields when you get near them. So, that said, we have boxes of silly string to find the mine fields. The mines can be set off with a cell phone. Interestingly, the people who live here know to avoid certain areas. So they know, but they will not tell."

April looked at Sal and asked, "Will you give me a week's time to develop a good relationship with the locals. There has to be someone I can win over."

Sal replied. "You are the boss on this mission. We are to assist you."

April was a bit taken back. She was never in charge of a unit before. Her surprise did not show. She showed experience and confidence. "Okay. I will go about and see what I can find."

April changed into U.S. fatigues and with a scout began her walk into the village of this remote area. There were wild, skinny dogs running about. Some followed them hoping for a hand out. It was the same with children following them or running alongside for the same reason. April did have some candy in her pocket and put some in their hands. As they walked April noticed a boy about age nine and asked about him.

His known name was Remi. He was an orphan living in the streets. In the past the soldiers had used Remi for information, but then Remi would disappear for days.

As they walked, Remi followed along, dodging in and out of partially standing building. Some of the locals welcomed them in for tea, and April bowed to them with her hands folded to thank them. She learned nothing. April did have training in the language, which was not difficult. But all the villagers wanted to talk about was food, money, who was sick, or who died. They were too afraid to say anything else.

As they left one particular house, April stood back motioning for her scout to continue when she saw Remi dart looking for her, As he passed along the back wall, April reached out and grabbed him. Remi began to scream, and April covered his mouth shushing him to calm down. When he stopped screaming, April let him stand on his own, free. Remi looked ready to bolt when April leaned against the partial wall extending her hand to him with a piece of candy in it. Remi took the candy and smiled. That was the beginning of a valuable friendship.

Remi was an informant, a carefully watched informant. He had to be careful, and April understood that. So, she left him alone, and only under the cover of night did Remi come to their camp or meet secretly, sometimes far from camp. Each time April was there with food, fruit, or vegetables. It was obvious the boy was hungry, starving for food. April learned a lot. She asked Remi if he could draw a diagram showing to the best of his knowledge where the mines were.

He said both he and his brother had watched the enemy plant them. Unbeknownst to the enemy they had made a diagram on a nearby tree showing where each bomb was set in relation to each bunker.

"You know where the bunkers are?" April asked Remi, and he shook his head yes. "I have not seen your brother," April told him.

Remi looked sad and turned his hands upside down, indicating no more. His brother was no more.

April put her head down when she looked up she had tears in her eyes.

Remi stood suddenly and came towards April. Using his dirty hands he wiped her tears away.

April instinctively hugged Remi and he melted to her. Here was this little 10-year-old boy who was helping them, risking his life, had no Mother or Father, and no other siblings. They were all gone, dead. If he or she was not very careful, he would be dead too.

April addressed her concerns to Sal. "Yes, this is an unfortunate truth to war," Sal said. That did not set right with April.

With the information Remi had provided April set out with eleven other soldiers to the bunker on horseback. These were well-bred Arabian horses, trained for war. Their sure-footed feet did not sink or slip in the sand. When they arrived at the first bunker, April and Sal worked together to lay out the map on the ground as to where the bombs were. This was risky to depend on memory and writing skills of nine- and twelve-year-old boys. April sighed, she took the steps to what was an outer bomb and sprayed silly string, and sure enough there appeared a string like wire connecting to others. To detonate this would create a major hole, alerting everyone, but there was no other way. She radioed the Army base their findings and backed off.

Within a half hour a troop with hummers showed up, they had a field mine expert with them who also said, all or none. They all backed up four hundred yards or more and one shot on the spot they marked ignited all the bombs blowing a quarter-mile-deep hole in the sand.

As they neared the door of the bunker, which was as big as a barn with doors forty feet high and twenty feet wide. Sal was concerned there would be mine fields at the door. And he was right. As those mines were detonated that door busted open. That door was similar in thickness to a bank vault door. It was an amazing feat of craftsmanship. They all marveled at the work that would have entailed to build such a huge bunker. When they entered they knew why. There was machinery, tanks, hummers, cars, fake IDs, cell phones, computers, laptops, boxes and crates of rifles, and all amounts of coins in boxes. It was astounding. As big as this bunker was, things were squeezed in, and many things hung from the ceiling. April scooped up a handful of the coins putting them in her belly pouch which was seen by a soldier.

"You can't take that," he told her.

April mounted her mare. "Soldier do you know who I am?" she asked him.

With a lackadaisical stature and attitude, like he didn't care, he simply shrugged his shoulders.

April was immediately angry. "Stand at attention when I talk to you," she barked. "I am Officer D. You do not need to know my rank, just know that I am in charge of this mission. The U.S. Army responds to MY call, not the other way around. I suggest you recheck your attitude and leave it in your tent when you go out on a mission. You have a sloppy attitude, and I will not tolerate it," she told him.

April then rode to the officer that came with this unit and told him what had happened. "He has been here for eighteen months straight," he replied.

"I don't care how long he has been here. He needs to straighten up and fly straight. Do you understand me?" she asked angrily. "Our lives are at risk out here. He should know better."

Excuses, that is what everyone wanted to offer when they would not accept responsibility for their actions. She was sick of it. Yes, this did happen state side too, but she had no authority to correct it there. But here she did.

"We were told we are not allowed to take souvenirs," that officer said.

"This is not a souvenir. It is life, to buy food for the people it was stolen from," April replied. She got off her mare and took two more handfuls, putting them in her now over-stuffed pouch.

"Make sure you put this in your report, Officer. And spell my name right, APRIL D."

Sal sat on his horse. He turned his head to laugh. He did not want anyone to see him. This officer had spunk and they rightly had been served a heaping dose of reality.

On the way back the horses were restless and wanted to run. So, April let her mare's reins loose and they took off. She was not the fastest of the horses, but steady and reliable. It reminded her of home, of all the times she rode. She missed riding and was reminded how lucky she was to be here with an equestrian unit.

Back at camp with horses in place, April and Sal walked to the one village home that had welcomed them. There April gave two thirds of the pouch of money to be distributed to the people. They told this family they were in charge, to take care of the others, and to be careful. Food, glorious food was now within their reach. It was such a blessing. Many were grateful for her secret help.

Later Remi wandered into camp. April noticed blood marks on his wrists. She asked him what had happened, and he made his hands swipe together as if brushing cracker crumbs. He meant nothing, but it was obvious Remi had been captured, tied, and probed for answers.

April was upset.

Sal was concerned that April did not understand the ways of the enemy or their life here.

"You're right. I don't," April said. "It is impossible for me to understand. Is it all right to kill parents and your siblings in the name of war? Men are to fight war, not children. How messed up this is? If it were in my power, I would take him home to a normal life."

"He would like that, but his family would be killed." Sal answered.

"What family?" April asked.

Sal shook his head. He did not know. He did not know how to extract someone from here. It was true this boy had no one. And the horrors he had seen, lived with, and slept in fear, was no life.

In time, with Remi's help, eleven bunkers were found. After the last one, as they were riding back, their small band of rider's encountered enemy choppers who began firing on them. The horses were trained to run to places to block bullets, like trees and sand hills. But, as they ran, they were soon out in the open desert.

The choppers deployed heat-seeking missiles. The horses would run until the missiles were close by then lay down suddenly from a dead run. The missiles would fly over them, detonating in a hillside. But then, one missile turned and hit the chopper that had fired it. The chopper exploded in midair. That was an adrenalin pumping time. That was the last time the enemy appeared. Either they felt defeated, had problems elsewhere, or felt there was nothing here for them anymore. Even the villagers were more relaxed. Remi seemed less stressed.

What About Remi?

ONE EVENING APRIL SOUGHT OUT REMI AND ASKED HIM MANY questions. "Do you want to stay here? What will you do for a job to make money? Where will you get an education? Who will help you?" And lastly, "Do you want to come to the US with me to my home?"

Remi began to cry. "I come with you," he said over and over. Remi hugged her like she was his mother.

April had made up her mind. She was not going to leave unless this little guy was going with her. She had no transfer papers. She had nothing of the sort, but he was going home with her.

All seemed well. April had been here four weeks. The US troops that assisted in the mission, some were elsewhere, and some waited on their long-awaited trip home for R & R.

April was not going with them. Her ride was on the chopper that brought her. It was about noon. April was packed and waiting for Remi, but he was nowhere to be seen. Finally she sent a scout to the village and within minutes she heard her ride coming in. The chopper set down but did not shut off. They were eager to go to another drop site. As April walked to the chopper covering her face, she saw Remi out of the corner of her eye. She threw her bag on board and ran to Remi. She took a towel from the scout, covered Remi's head from the swirling sand, and pushed him aboard.

"Whoa. Whoa. We can't take him along," the pilot said.

"No, you can't, but I can," she said. It's my souvenir. Carry on. Let's go home," and she looked at Remi with tears running down his face, his eyes lit up with hope.

They flew for two hours straight into Germany. There April and Remi went into a station and April was looking keenly for someone. She found what she was looking for, a shyster. Someone who could make a fake passport and birth certificate for Remi. He would be her nephew. It cost her 150.00 U.S. dollars. When the passport and papers were in her hand, she silently thanked God. Yes, she lied, but she lied to save him. She lied to take him home where he would finally have a life.

She had some spare time to spend in Germany, two days. So they both got something to eat and a hotel room. Remi was amazed at all of the modern conveniences. His village did not have running water. He ate like he never ate before. April was concerned he would gorge himself and become sick.

They then went to a phone kiosk to call her Mom. The connection was not very good there was a lot of static. April would hold her finger in her ear to block out the noise. And just like everyone else she would yell into the phone receiver.

Miranda was confused when April said she was bringing her nephew home. From what April described, he was living in deplorable conditions with no parents. Her daughter asked if Dad could fly down and pick up the boy as she was not free to leave her base.

Miranda was thinking what to do. She was currently cat sitting for Lena and June, which Ruby was extremely unhappy about. She knew Gordon would not have any time off just now. She thought and thought, then she asked if it mattered who picked him up.

April replied, "No, so long as he gets home."

Miranda asked April to call back in two hours and hung up the telephone to call her husband to explain the situation.

He asked if she could call John and Betty. They might enjoy the trip to Florida.

And then Miranda remembered Mel and Tina. They lived in Florida, and she was sure they would help them out. So she dialed their number, and Tina answered.

"Hello, Tina. Why this is Miranda De Angelo in California." They talked for over a half hour before Miranda finally brought up the current problem.

"I know Mel would go. He loves to travel, and you know Mel, he does not take guff from anyone. I am still not doing so well with my leg. It is much better, but I cannot walk far like in airport terminals. I hope you understand. But I am sure Mel will do it. I will call you back shortly," and she did. The plan was set in motion. Mel had already purchased a ticket and would be in Florida tomorrow. He would wait for April to call him. He had left his cell number via Tina with Miranda.

Miranda fretted walking back and forth waiting and hoping that April would call. April did, and the arrangements were made. April had Mel's cell number and it was a go. From there Mel would leave Florida, fly with Remi, and bring him home. Oh, if only she would have had some notice. Miranda was more than happy to pay for the flight tickets. She hated to ask anyone, but for right now she was stuck.

When Gordon came home, he got the news of the itinerary. "It should work. I know you hated to ask, but it will be nice to see Mel again."

"I wish Tina could come along too, but it's understandable. And I wonder what happened to this boy's parents, and nephew."

That night the two of them pondered what was going to happen. With April you never knew, and then they fell asleep.

April and Remi boarded their flight from Germany to her base in Florida. She had all of Remi's papers in hand, as well as his passport. When she landed, her Commanding Officer was there waiting to see her. "Oh, boy," she said to herself. "That man never waited to see anyone. They always had to run when he said run." she figured she would be either in trouble, discharged, called out and cussed at, or maybe all of the above.

She and Remi entered the office, and April told Remi to wait there. He looked panicked as she left, but April reassured Remi he would be all right. Inside the Commander's office, however, it was not all right. He was very upset, and when very upset, he screamed not talked.

"I sent you there to do a job, not play nurse maid. What in the hell got into your mind? Do you know the international trouble you are in for this? I am in for this?" He went on and on, and then April asked for permission to speak freely.

"Sir, I did as you asked. The bunkers were all found, but not by me, or anyone from the U.S. It was that little boy out there. He and his murdered brother, who was twelve, had made a map of where the bombs were planted. He was the informant, Sir. Do you know what would have become of him?" she yelled back.

"I don't give a damn what would have become of him. Don't you understand?" he spewed.

April blew up. "No, Sir. I do not understand. When did you get so darn cold? Or are all of us so expendable, not worth the dirt on your shoe. He is a little boy, a frightened little boy. You want me to fight a war for you? Good. I will go wherever you ask me too. I am an adult. He is nine. Just nine years old. You have a son that is thirteen. Would you leave him behind in a war-torn country where it would be likely for him to be killed?"

"Don't talk so dumb," he said to her. "My son has nothing to do with this boy."

April reeled, "Seriously, nothing? You consider your thirteen-year-old son better than this boy, when this boy could make maps of bombs. He lived three years without any parents, fending for himself and hiding from the enemy. Could your son do that?"

"D, you're treading on thin ground," he said.

"Ice. You mean ice, and you may be right. Know this, I would not have been able to fulfill this mission without that boy. You can court martial me, throw me in the brig, or give me a dishonorable discharge. It is your decision, but I am standing here to tell you that boy is not going back. He has nothing and no one to go back to. My parents will give him what he needs. They did for me, and I stand on that. I would love to have your wife's input on this matter since you value her thoughts so much."

April's chest was heaving slightly, and her heart was racing. Damn she was angry. In her head she kept thinking, chose your battles carefully. He was her Commanding Officer, and she was sassing him.

He, on the other hand, felt April had stuck a dagger in his heart. If his wife had been sitting here, she would take the boy in. They only had one son. They were not able to have more children and she spoke often of adoption.

He was not going to take backtalk from her or anyone else. He looked at her and shouted "Dismissed."

April saluted him and left closing the door harder than ever before behind her. She came out and gathered Remi who studied her with questions in his eyes. She headed to the outpost and signed out. She and Remi were now off base for three days. And she was going to show him some fun in the event he might have to go back to that hell hole he came from.

April's Commanding Officer sat in his office stewing. No soldier ever spoke to him as she did, but he let her. Why? Because he saw in her an honest, hardworking, give-it-all-you-got soldier heaving in anger. He never saw her like that before. She was always so agreeable, went on every mission they asked of her, and she was successful, cunning and came out with what they wanted. He sighed. Oh hell, who would know. The kid did not have anyone. He leaned forward and pressed the intercom button requesting his secretary to come to him.

When she got to his door, he said, "Find me some way to get papers for that kid to stay stateside. Ask a jag attorney if needed but keep it quiet. He has no one and no one is going to look for or ask about him.".

"Well, Sir. He had a passport and papers with him."

The Commander sat there reeling at how prepared April was. She was dead serious about this boy going home with her and made the paperwork appear, illegal but he would have to produce papers as well. "Just do your best and let me know in the morning." He got up and left.

When he got home that evening, as he and his wife sat together on their couch, she asked him what was bothering him. He began to explain, and she began to cry.

"Oh, Honey, now don't cry," he said to her.

She looked at him with tears in her eyes. "Oh, Harlan. I have known you all my life and you know I have a soft spot for children. How could you have been so cold when she was only trying to help the boy. What if it had been our boy?"

"Oh, not you too," he said as he got up from the couch upset.

"Harlan, you come back here," she said to him. He did and she lovingly got up and hugged him. "I know you will do the right thing, Dear. You always do. That is why I am so very proud of you."

The Commander was notified that April was off base for three days, which was her right. He put a call into her cell phone. When she did not answer, he sent MPs to find her. Within an hour she was sitting at his desk.

"Here are some papers for you that you will need for the boy."

April looked at them. They looked official, professionally done, and there on the bottom was her Commanding Officer's signature. April stood up and felt like crying, "Permission to kiss your cheek, Sir."

His face flushed, but he did not refuse her.

April felt like skipping down the hallway. She met Remi who was sitting in the MP's jeep asking hundreds of questions.

"Your nephew sure is curious," he said.

"Yes, he is a very bright boy," April said.

Within an hour April received a text message from Mel. He was on his way and would arrive in about an hour. April was able to sit Remi down and tell him about his journey, and that he was to trust people. It was not like Iraq. She told him about her parents and Monte, the horses and ponies, the dairy, and the people back home. Remi absorbed the information like a smiling sponge. Soon Mel was there, and he took Remi's hand, and they left like old pals. Mel talking and Remi asking questions.

As the days dwindled down, word spread about what April did. Sergeant Bob came to talk to her. "That is a damn wonderful thing you did. There are thousands of kids that will not get the chance that he did. He is one lucky boy."

April agreed and asked that he pray for Remi so he could adjust.

"Adjust? That boy is going to be in heaven," he said.

Then she took Sergeant Bob's hand, "I want to thank you for your help, guidance and friendship here. You have helped me in every way." Bob hugged her and that was the last time April saw Sergeant Bob.

Mel was home with Remi and the two of them spent time with Tina. She was so impressed at how polite and kind Remi was. Tina called Miranda to tell her. She said Mel and Remi would be there tomorrow.

As she hung up the telephone, Miranda began to feel those maternal instincts. "Oh, come on now old girl. You are too old to be a mother, again!"

But he did come to their home and Remi loved Gordon as much as any boy could love a father. He idolized him. Miranda he treated like a queen, running for anything she wanted or needed. That is how it was for all of his growing years.

Remi excelled in school in both science and engineering. He decided he would go to college one day and be an engineer and build amazing things, and he did. He blessed the Di Angelo house for eleven years. His photos were hung beside April's. Yes, Remi Di Angelo received a family, a mother, a father, and a sister, as well as an entire town who loved and respected him. He did much more than he ever hoped for, and he told everyone that was the key to happiness. Always be happy with what you have.

In tribute to Remi who served valiantly in the Iraq war from 2004 to 2010 and lost. A huge "Thank You" to a brave young man. You are not forgotten.

Her remaining days in the military were becoming fewer and fewer. April was restless. The running and exercises were not enough. Her mind raced. She wondered how Remi was adjusting to home, how her parents were, and she longed to go home. It was a matter of days, but you never know when you are owned by the military.

A week later her review and subsequent discharge papers arrived. The Commander tried to convince her how much she was needed, but her mind was made up.

"Sir, I have given my best in every mission and here on base. I am done, finished. I want to go home." Her papers were stamped "Honorable Discharge", her flight was booked, and four days later April D was heading home.

She did not remember that flight. It was such a relief, letting go, and relaxing. She slept most of the flight.

April touched down in Georgia. It was a layover. She looked around and found a shop with magazines and newspapers. She bought a paper and sat at her boarding area reading, devouring the pages. April was hungry to return to civilization.

Soon she was boarding. Many reached to shake her hand, to thank her. It was a very humbling experience. In her seat, ready for takeoff, she closed her eyes, and said a prayer of thanks to her Father in Heaven. She made it safely out after two years and eight months of service. She was going home and in her mind she could recall the many others who never got to go home, and she wept. No one said a word to her, either they did not notice, or they let her to her privacy. It was a sobering ride of thoughts, contemplation, and soul searching. It seemed a short ride when she heard the Captain of the plane announce they would be touching down at the Fresno airport.

She had little gear to bring along, just a bag in steerage, so she sat there waiting like all the other passengers. Just then a man sitting behind her tapped her shoulder. She turned partially when the man whispered to her, "Thank you for your service to our country." That almost set April to tears again, but she composed herself extending her hand to shake his.

The plane was dead still on the tarmac, and the passengers were about to exit the plane when the Captain came on the loud speaker again. "Ladies and Gentlemen we have a special passenger on board today and I am asking that you give this one soldier the special privilege of leaving our plane first."

April stood up and they began to clap. She could not hold back her tears, over and over she repeatedly said, "Thank you" to them.

Some reached to shake her hand and at the exit the Captain was there to shake her hand too. April thought if every soldier was shown appreciation like this. It would prove to them how thankful citizens were for their protection.

Down the ramp she went, when she saw her parents and many of her friends and neighbors from home. Some of the ground crew shook her hand. As she walked to her group those waiting for another passenger joined April's group, wanting to thank her.

April reached for her Dad, Mom, and Remi. It was a sea of tears all around, happy tears. She was home! After a half hour of her meeting all of them, she left to get her bag and they left the airport.

On the ride home her Dad kept looking in the mirror and her Mother kept looking in the back seat. Remi was there sitting beside April holding onto her hand. Yes, it was good to be home. She had her whole life to plan and decide what to do, it was time.

Home at last

AT HOME SHE PACKED HER THINGS IN HER ROOM. SHE LOOKED around and Mom had changed her sewing room into a room for Remi. It was a cool room. It had a race track on the floor near the bottom of his bed and shelves that had model cars and things he built. His closet held nice school clothing and his hall tree held barn clothing. Yes sir, he was home! April was happy.

The telephone rang and soon Remi called to her. "It's for you," he said.

She took the receiver and said, "Hello?"

"Hello, April. Welcome Home." It was Mr. Stevens. "Is there any way for you to drop by, say maybe tomorrow?"

"Oh, I am sure there is. Is there a problem?" April asked.

"No, but there is a development I want to talk to you about. I think you would be interested, but we need to act quickly," he said.

"Okay. Well, I will stop tomorrow, and we can have lunch at the diner."

"That would be really nice. I will see you at Flo's Diner at lunchtime tomorrow," he confirmed.

"Yes. See you then, and thank you for calling," April said and then hung up the receiver.

"Something going on?" her Mother asked.

"I don't know. I will meet with him tomorrow and find out then. For now I am going to not worry about a thing," and she bear hugged her Mother who screamed which set Ruby to barking and Remi laughing.

"So, young man. What are your jobs here at home?" April asked Remi.

"Not much. I do little things," he said.

"Oh, he does much more than that," Miranda added. "He takes the trash out, feeds the ponies, works in the garden, and helps Daddy working on the truck or around the farm."

"Oh, so now you have my jobs," April tickled him teasing him. Remi wiggled on the couch laughing trying to escape her grasp.

He stood up with a huge grin, "I fit in."

"Yes, you do, like a glove," Miranda said.

Miranda stepped forward hugging Remi and planted a kiss on his forehead. "Such a handsome young man. Don't you think so, April?"

"Oh, yes. I do," April said. "He is going to be someone's heart break someday."

"I will not. I am never getting married," Remi said.

During her days of nothing to do, she and Remi had many conversations about family, church, and they developed a real sibling bond. He really was a good boy, grateful for a second chance. But April wanted him to let that go and be one with their family. She felt that in time his past would melt away. The more he was loved, the more he would forget.

The next day April met with Mr. Stevens, who was already at the diner with spread sheets laid out on the back table. April came in with the doorbell dinging.

"Oh, mercy sakes. Look what the cat drug in," Flo said coming to hug her. They were all so kind and loving to her. She thought back to her long relationship with them since age five. To her they too were family.

She then sat down with Mr. Stevens who also hugged her. "Welcome home," he said.

They had a light lunch as Mr. Stevens laid out a plan to see if April was interested. He said, "Right now D Farms owned no less than three farms in each state in the US. Some states had six or more." Most were dairy farms, but he diversified in the south with produce and peanut farms.

He told April there was a large span of land for sale in Hawaii. He said it would be good for her to see the property, on topical maps it looked more than suitable. It would be a sizable market as there were no dairies in Hawaii.

April was interested. "So, when do you want to go?" she asked him.

"I thought the sooner the better. I would like for your parents to go, their son of course, and perhaps the Marshalls," he said.

"The Marshalls?" April questioned him.

"Well, yes. I know Hugh is trying to work things out with you and it would give you a good opportunity to see how he is in public."

April was about to protest, but then she realized Mr. Stevens might have a point. She had not received one card or one letter, nothing from Hugh during her last year in the military. There had to be a reason. Perhaps it would come out on this trip.

April stood up and shook Mr. Steven's hand. "I will try to make arrangements with my parents and the Marshalls as soon as possible and then call you. I think your idea is an excellent one," and she winked at him.

"Yes, I want you to be cautious. It is not how it seems," he said. "I have heard things, but then you know talk is cheap. I think we need to see with our own eyes, so to speak."

April thanked him again, hugged him, and left with Flo calling after her to come back real soon.

April did not resist the urge she had to go and see Native Son. When she arrived at the stable, he was outside in the pasture. She called to him. He perked up his ears and ran to her. She shook her head in dismay at how much that horse knew her and loved her. He came to the rail of the fence and put his big head over to greet her. She held onto it placing her head on his. The two of them stayed that way for a while. April swore she could feel his thought and he felt hers. She walked to the top gate with him walking on the fence side beside her. Native Son had a rug on to keep his sleek condition.

She unbuckled the clasps, pushed the rug off, and hopped on. He looked at her and just stood there. April leaned forward and laid over his body to his neck, just petting his neck and talking smoothly to him. Love is the greatest power on this earth, and these two knew it. She spent more time there than she planned, but she was not sorry. She had been away from him for a long three plus years.

As she was about to leave, a large hay truck came rambling into the driveway and her truck was blocking it. She called out to the driver to wait a minute while she hurried to move the truck. Monte came out and directed the driver to the back of the barn. April followed them. As they walked April asked Monte who the man was. She was told he was a farmer from over the valley. Monte was buying his hay as it was of much better quality than he bought previously.

April walked up to introduce herself and the man ignored her. April was surprised.

"He is not standoffish. He is just shy," Monte whispered to her. As the two men were talking about the hay, when it was cut, the condition, and so on, April forcefully walked forward taking the man's hand in hers to introduce herself. "Hello. I am April D," but the man did not answer. His face just blushed red, and he stammered.

Monte swore to this day that when April took his hand, there were sparks, then he came to the rescue. "Larry, this is April. She owns Native Son and most of the horses here. She just returned home recently."

"Oh," Larry said. "Do you live around here or work here?" he asked.

"Well, right now I do. I just got home from the military and am deciding what to do." She studied the man and found herself thinking he is a handsome man, quiet, calm, and patient. "Next time when you deliver hay, if you have some time to spare, I can show you around at some of our farms in this area," she said to the man.

"I would like that," he replied.

For some reason her heart leapt, totally unexpectedly and she felt unsure why.

"Okay," the man said. "I will be back in two weeks with another load." He looked at April. "I'll take you out for some lunch and we can take that trip to look around if you like."

April was dumbfounded and unable to find her tongue. In her mind she knew they might be in Hawaii and might not be back, and again it was Monte to the rescue.

"We will be here. Just make time to be able to stay for a while."

The man got in his truck and looked at April. All she could do was smile. She felt like a dummy. How embarrassing.

When the man left, April knew she should go too, but Monte was at her shoulder, "Now there is a good man for you April. He is a crop farmer. He has a large span of land right near here, not too far from home. He is a quiet man. I have known him for ten years or so. I knew his parents. A nice guy, a hard worker, polite, and kind. You could not ask for more," he said.

April just wanted to go home and escape. Everyone was trying to hook her up and get her married.

At home her Mother asked where she had been, and April told her. "Oh, I met Larry several times. He is a really nice man," but that is all she said.

April sighed. She just wanted to live for a little bit. Was that asking too much? She wanted to wait until dinner when Dad was home to discuss Mr. Steven's plans.

Dad looked at the calendar on the wall, "I can go this week or the week after. There is not much going on," he said.

She asked her Dad if he would extend the call to the Marshall's at Mr. Steven's request, and he did.

Mr. Marshall was confused at why Mr. Stevens wanted his family to go, but he loved to travel, and Hawaii always interested him. Besides he and Elaine had not had a vacation in quite some time. Why not? He just needed to check with Hugh first before he could answer. Mr. Marshall called later that evening and he said that so long as Hugh had enough notice, he could take some time off. But no more than three days.

April called Mr. Stevens and gave him the information. He told her that he could book tickets for all of them to leave in three days. He had found a site online that listed flight, hotel, and all accommodations for lower prices. The site "filled in" if they had empty rooms and offered them at lower prices.

"Awesome," April said to him. So her family of four, the Marshalls family of four, and the Stevens family of two would be a total of ten. Three days later they were all standing in the airport to board their flight to Hawaii. Hugh was nervous and spent a lot of time talking privately with his Mother. April was relaxed and happy taking a vacation with her family was awesome. She knew neither her Mom, Dad, she, Rami, Lena, and June had never been to Hawaii. It would be a new experience for them all.

The seating was difficult because Hugh insisted he sit with April. So April took Rami in hand with him sitting between her and Hugh. She explained to Hugh that Rami felt unsure, and it would be comforting to him if the both of them made him feel special, included. Rami went along with the ruse. He liked it now. He was able to talk to Hugh and April. April liked the distance. She could ask Hugh questions without him being defiant or powerful over her. Her Mother and Dad were behind her with Trevor. Mr. Stevens sat with his son and Lena behind her parents. The Marshalls and June sat behind the Stevens. It all worked out fine.

At their hotels, Hugh thought he and April could share a room. At which April was aghast. "Are you nuts?" she said.

"It's not about intimacy or having sexual relations. I want to get to know you again," he protested.

April was not happy. How dare he make that decision. After all was not a luncheon date good enough?

It was a bad start, and when the arrangements were made to see the property, over 2,900 acres, Hugh was undecided if he wanted to go. April didn't care anymore. Hugh was acting spoiled. Elaine approached April and explained that Hugh took off four days to spend with her, not his parents or brother. If she would just make time and space for Hugh.

Did they not get that she was here to buy property? But April said she would for Elaine's sake and rolled her eyes. Remi laughed at her. He understood what was going on. He was no dummy.

Miranda was clueless, but it was Dad, from information from his buddy Remi who came to April. "Honey you do what you want. I don't understand what is going on. Why is Hugh trying to be forceful with you? Just do what you want and feel comfortable with. If you need me, I am here."

April loved her Dad so much. The "if you need me, I am here," touched her heart. She never told her Dad about her missions and what she was capable of, she could really take care of herself, but she loved him for it.

They all arrived at the meeting point about the same time. There were horses to ride to see the entire property, which most was wooded.

April helped Remi who was quite adapt at riding. They were all mounted when the two scouts headed out. It was early, about eight in the morning. They went down into a valley. It was thick with trees and brush. The horses were careful and went slowly. On the flat of the land the scouts showed Mr. Stevens the fertile land and pointed to a lake that was on the property with large streams. None of the property was overly wet unless they went to the coast line.

April was impressed. This land was breathtaking. Her Mother and the Ladies were in complete agreement with her. Mr. Stevens pointed out vantage points where a building could be, there was water access, and the land was lush and level.

April's Dad wondered if there were wild animals that would interfere and asked what danger there was. When the land is clean those threats would be removed. Her Dad was no fool. He knew that animals had territories, and he said that it would take time to remove them, to take them far away, or kill the threats that lived there, and the scouts agreed. They rode around the entire property line and cut through the middle to make faster time back.

Hugh rode beside April often and asked her to stop being so distracted and to listen to him. He asked her what her decision was.

April held her horse and said, "Hugh, I just got back two days ago and now we are here. And you want me to soul search my feelings and decide how I feel about you?"

"Yes, I do," he said to her.

"What is your hurry?" April asked him.

Hugh's face flushed. "There is no hurry. I just want an answer," he replied.

"Well, I don't have one right now. How about we make time for a lunch tomorrow and discuss this and get to the heart of the problem?" she pushed back.

Hugh defensively said, "Okay, tomorrow, lunch, and then I have to go back."

Miranda caught wind of their conversation and asked April what happened. When April explained the look in Miranda's eyes changed. "You go and find out. There has to be something going on that he is pressing you for time," she said. "Maybe he is going on a dangerous mission or maybe he has things to resolve."

"Yes, and maybe he is involved with someone again," April said. No more was said. April was thinking of lunch tomorrow. She had to get away somewhere to have prayer alone, in the quiet. She needed help.

That evening after they all decided to go out to dinner hosted by Mr. Marshall, April opted to go with Mr. Stevens to meet the owners of the property and discuss terms.

They met in a very small cabana. The owners were a lovely, older couple. They wanted to sell their property and move stateside to where their son and daughter were. They felt isolated, alone here in Hawaii. They said they inherited this property from parents, and it had always been in their family. They did not want their land developed with skyscrapers and vacationers. Their ancestors were farmers. That was the reason they talked to Mr. Stevens. He and April honestly laid out the plans they had. The couple had a few suggestions with what would work best from their experience.

Mr. Stevens looked at April, "What do you think?" he asked her.

"I love the property. It would provide jobs and a viable living for people here on the island. There would be milk and meat for those living here. There would be trucks to take the milk to a ship for transport. That would be the only concern, really.

The couple was satisfied. The agreement was signed, and Mr. Stevens wrote out a whopping check. The couple told him over and over that he could make payments.

"No," he said. "D Farms always pays their bills." They said their goodbyes and parted way. On the way out, Mr. Stevens said, "Now you own a huge chunk of Hawaii."

It all seems surreal to April. She turned and hugged Mr. Stevens. "D Farms would not have much of anything without you. I want you to know you and your family are always welcome here whenever you want."

He stood there and admitted his wife lamented of wanting to come along. "You can bring her on our private jet. You know that," April told him.

"Yes. I know, but I hate to take from the company," he told her. Mr. Stevens was an honest business man. He had come from humble beginnings and never changed.

They headed back to the hotel. April went into her room and flopped on her bed. She sure missed Ruby. She found herself thinking about the man she met at Monte's. She would much rather have lunch with him than Hugh. April was insistent she never wanted to be owned, that is not love. Love is letting that person free to make choices, then they want to return.

Soon everyone was back. Her Father and Mr. Marshall were anxious to know what April decided.

"It's ours," she said with a smile.

They both laughed shaking each other's hands, "I would bring some angus to roam these woods for you," Mr. Marshall joked.

Then Hugh came in wanting to know what happened. "You bought it, just like that?" he asked. "I would have to work for sixty years or more to buy land like that," he mused.

April walked out of the room. Surely by now Hugh knew that she did not outright own any of the farms on D Farms. It was a cooperation. Her name was on it, and yes invested by each farm, but she herself did not buy this land. April began to think Hugh wanted her for her money and that was a joke.

She found her Mother with Rami, Mrs. Marshall, and the Ladies in the boutique in the hotel. Rami wanted a sweatshirt that he carried. April told him when he was old enough and wanted to earn his way in college, he could come here to Hawaii to work and live.

"Really?" he asked her.

"Yes, absolutely. Many others have earned their education like that. If you want to live in Hawaii there is no reason why you can't."

Rami put the sweatshirt back and said, "I don't need it. I will live here one day and wish for D Farms shirts," and they laughed, and she hugged him. April picked up a lanyard for him to keep keys on. He like it. Miranda could not resist a pair of earrings and Elaine bought a bracelet.

"April come and pick something out," her Mother said.

April but her arms around both of the women and said, "I want these," and the women laughed. The Ladies bought long nightshirts that April insisted she pay for. They hugged her and met up with the others.

Nighttime came and April was restless. She did not want tomorrow to come. She began to dread time with Hugh. Miranda was wide awake. She could not sleep. Something was bothering her daughter and it bothered her. She got up and walked down the hall to April's door and knocked. "It's Mom."

April walked and opened the door.

"I wanted to come in. I can't sleep," her Mother said.

"What, too much riding?" April asked her.

Miranda sat on the edge of April's bed. She slapped the bed motioning for April to sit beside her. "Your hair is growing longer," as she stroked her daughters hair. "Talk to me, Sweetie. I know something is wrong," she said to April.

April looked at her Mother and said, "Mom I don't want to hurt your feelings."

Miranda kissed her daughter's cheek, "You never have hurt or disappointed me, dear. Now talk to your Mother."

April sighed, "Mom, I know you and Dad have strong feeling for Hugh to be with me, but I don't. I gave Hugh a year to see if he would be faithful. Do you remember when right before I left we went to dinner at the country club. Do you remember? That is when Hugh asked me to go outside, he begged me to give him a second chance, and I agreed. The whole year and eight months before I was discharged I did not get one letter or post card from Hugh, not one text message on my cell. Tomorrow he wants to talk to me. He is pushy, and I am beginning to believe he is after money not me."

Miranda pressed her daughter's head to her chest. "Stop worrying. I can feel you're anxiousness. Stop it. You are a strong woman. I know you had to be, for I know you faced many enemies on your mission from people who wanted to take your life. You stood your ground and did what you had to do. You have already experienced the worst from Hugh. If you have a bad feeling, walk away. You should never settle, dear, not for Hugh or anyone. His family loves you weather you are with Hugh or not. So make your decision for you. You would be the one to live with him, not any of us."

April loved her Mother, finally she felt what April was feeling and she hugged her Mom. The next day at lunch April felt much better. She met Hugh and together they walked to a place for lunch. It was a good long walk that gave them time to talk.

Hugh seemed different, like the old Hugh, but April knew tigers do not change their stripes. We are what we are. At lunch April ordered crab cakes and a salad, she felt bad for the little crabs, but she dearly loved their taste.

They talked and Hugh pressed April about where she could live, not on base, but somewhere in between so he could pop in when he was off. He asked if she would take care of little Michael so they would be a family. Hugh was concerned about the cost of a home and living expenses and wondered if the corporation would support them.

April stared at him incredibly shocked. He gave no consideration to his Mother's feelings of losing Michael, or that April might want an education. And was she not ready to be a mother. Why should his mistake become her job?

"Hugh, don't you think I should pursue an education?" she asked him.

"Well, after Michael is grown. Right now he should be the priority. Don't you agree?"

"For you, yes, but not for me," she said. "I just came off of a four plus years of harrowing missions and I'm not ready to jump into marriage or motherhood. I believe I deserve time for my education. I earned that. Don't you think so?" she questioned.

"I thought you were trained to go into motherhood and have a lot of children," he said to her.

"Hugh, I am not a pioneer. I have worked all my life building up farms for the good of others. You know that. So don't you think now that I am twenty-one, I am ready for my own education and to pursue my own goals? You did. Why can't I?" April pressed him.

"Because I am the man. I make the bread and take care of the family," Hugh said.

April reeled. What a sexist comment, yet here he was asking if the corporation could help them with housing and living expenses.

April looked at Hugh. "What is this about, really?" she asked him.

Hugh looked at her like she was daft. "April, I need to make concrete plans. I want a mother for Michael, and I need a wife. April, I have needs."

"Like I don't. Where were your letters, postcards, calls, or text messages in the last year and eight months? You expect me to turn on when you appear?"

April laid her fork down. She was done. "Hugh, I am sorry, but I am not what you want or need. We have some things in common, but barely. I am never going to settle for any man. A man should be willing to walk on busted glass with his lips for the woman he loves. All I hear is 'It's all about you.' I will always look back on you as a friend. Go on with your life and be happy." She got up and walked out leaving Hugh sitting there speechless. Walking out she felt as if a weight had been lifted off her shoulders. She walked as if she was walking on air. If she missed anything at all, it would be those little crab cakes.

What's Next for April?

BACK AT THE HOTEL SHE TOLD HER PARENTS SHE WAS GOING TO FLY out with Mr. Stevens to return home on the private jet. Her parents thought that was a good idea, but the rest of them wanted to stay two more days and then return. April met Mr. Stevens and his son in the hotel foyer, they planned to leave that afternoon. At home he had to go to the bank and change around payments. As she sat there April decided that she would go to school in an accelerated program for veterinarian science.

So when her parents came home, she told them she would spend the summer here at home, apply at schools, and most likely leave in the fall. Her parents were in complete agreement.

Only her Dad asked about Hugh, and April said it was over. Gordon hugged his daughter, he prayed for her every morning and night.

Before the others came home, April found Ruby sleeping on the couch and scooped her up. She licked April everywhere she could, even with April telling her "no".

She sat there and got out her Mom's laptop and began looking at schools. She thought it would be good to go to the high school tomorrow, get her grade transcripts, and perhaps the guidance teacher could help her with applications.

She was excited. Her whole life lay out in front of her, and she could not wait. This was only the end of May. She had the next five months to work, ride, and enjoy those whom she loved before she set off for a career. Her heart was happy. She slid off of the couch to thank her Father in Heaven. That prayer was only a prayer of thanks, for the time she served, his warnings in dreams, the aid of others when she needed it, for Rami, and for helping her end whatever it was with Hugh. She could not think of one want in her life right now.

That summer she did meet with Larry. They had lunch and several dates. He had difficulty showing her that he cared for her in words, but he showed her in many other ways. When she asked him what he wanted as a small gift before she left for school, he looked at her and said, "All I want is You." She fainted inside. He was everything she could ask for in a man. He loved farming as much as she did. He was a hard worker. He loved animals. He was kind, thoughtful, polite, and April knew he liked her more than anyone. She would have said "love", but he never said that word. That was all right with her. Many say it, but don't show it.

Monte told her long ago that Larry was not like her people, meaning religious, but he was mistaken. Larry had a strong testimony of the Savior Jesus Christ. He did pray a lot, but not for anyone to hear. He did attend church with April and joined before she left for college. Not that she asked him to or made any ultimatum. When asked why he joined, he said, "If you sit there and listen long enough, you will know what is said is right." So, yes. Those two developed a wonderful, best friend relationship which made her parents happy.

For now the raking of hay, swimming, riding, and building relationships with Remi and Larry, as well as time with her parents and the Ladies, was almost at an end. Judge Du Val's wedding was one of the summer's highlights. April was in the wedding. Soon she would be packing to leave for college in Pittsburgh PA. Life was good. There was so much to look forward to including December break. There was so much good behind her. It was not as difficult saying goodbye this time. She knew, as they all did, that she would be home in December. With good news they hoped, grade wise.

She was taking a flight to school. She had no need for a car. The college was only eleven blocks from the zoo where she took a job to supplement her income. April said she would buy a bicycle and pedal back and forth or walk. It would be good exercise.

She did not take any money from the D Farm Corporation. She wanted to do this on her own, be independent.

April promised to write. So her mother personally bought a whole stack of stamped postcards and put them in her suitcase. She had minimal clothing she felt if she needed clothes she could buy them where she was, or Mom could send what she needed.

Before she knew it, she was having a last dinner with Larry. When he dropped her off at home, he had tears in his eyes. "Don't cry. I will be back home in December. You know I have four years to cram what I need into my noggin'," she joked as she tapped on her head.

Larry did not want to leave, and it broke her heart. She knew he had stronger feeling for her than he could say. "I promise to be your one and only. I will be back."

"That's good," he said wiping his tears away. They kissed, said goodbye, and he drove away. It had been a busy time for him, but he always made time to see her. And she loved to surprise him on his farm and help him with raking hay, cooking a meal, or with his animals. She sighed and went inside.

Her parents and Remi were sitting in the living room talking. It was rare for them to have the television on, unless for the news.

"Are you about ready?" her Mother asked.

"Yes, I am. It's not easy leaving you and I know I will be back in December. It's just, I don't know," she said.

"It will be all right," her Dad said. "School jitters, that's all it is."

"I hope so. I keep thinking I am forgetting something," she said. "Mom, I am letting my family genealogy with you. So keep it safe for me. I know June and Lena put a lot of travel and work into it, so you are in charge of it. Okay?"

"April, stop fretting. You know I will put it in a safe place. Come here and sit down."

April sat beside her Mother, and she felt silly. Here she was, a twenty-one-year-old, something was eating at her, and she did not know what it was. "Did you pray about it, Dear?" her Mother asked.

"Yes, I have, many times. It's like a bad feeling. I know school is good for me and I did not feel like this going on missions." She was agitated and confused. Her Dad suggested a Father's blessing.

Her Dad put a kitchen chair in the living room, and April sat down. They all showed reverence by folding their arms across their chest as her Father put his hands on his daughter's head and pronounced a blessing. It was a beautiful blessing, one of love, inspiration, and caution. He poured out his feeling to April of his Fatherly love for her. He reassured her that whatever she would be called to do or endure, her Father in Heaven would send angels to watch over and help her. Over and over the blessing expressed that she was to be careful, make assessments and wise choices, and to listen to warnings or her intuition.

When her Dad had finished, April hugged him and said, "I did not have that much apprehension from you about my military time," and she laughed. Her Dad on the other hand told her to try to remember that blessing. If not, she would suffer the consequences.

April knew all too well what he was talking about. She had witnessed others receive blessings only to make huge blunders, like Hugh did. "I will do my best, Sir," she said reassuring him.

But her Dad was not so easily convinced. He had that same foreboding she had, and it concerned him so much he suggested she take another flight. Perhaps it was a warning about the flight. So, the next morning Miranda made the change. April would not be leaving early in the morning. She was now leaving at 10:00 a.m. Her Dad felt better, but April did not tell them she had not slept that entire night. She hoped she could sleep on the plane.

The next morning her family drove her to the airport with her luggage which consisted of two bags: one held the books she had to have and read, and the other contained her clothing. She was anxious to go and felt so much better. She kissed them all goodbye and disappeared in the tunnel to board the airplane.

It was a nice flight, sunny and clear. The plane was half empty and April slept peacefully. At touchdown she gathered her two bags and walked out of the terminal.

She hailed a cab and it drove her right to the small apartment she had secured a month ago. It was a cozy little brick apartment between the college and the zoo. It had a small kitchen, a medium-sized living room, and a bedroom and bathroom upstairs. That was it, and she loved it. Her interior walls in the kitchen and living room were brick. The house was very old and only had one apartment. The neighbor on the other side of April's wall was her 86-year-old landlord. She was spry with a great mind.

April had little furniture. She did find a second-hand shop and purchased a large old table that looked like cherrywood. She wanted to use that for a desk so she could spread out her books and papers on it. She bought an old brass lamp with three settings. Her bed was a full size that she bought at a yard sale. It was a rope bed and she liked it. She did go to a store and buy towels, bedding, a comforter, and a pillow. For the living room she had a recliner that someone was giving away. It was an old La-Z-Boy that the handle had broken off. She was glad that her Dad had taught her to fix things. She bought a handle for it at a hardware store, and it worked out great. She also needed a chair to sit at the table, and her neighbor had several she could have. In return April fixed some meals for the elderly woman and in a short time the two became good friends. They often ate dinner or lunch together depending on April's class schedule and her job.

April loved, loved, loved her job. She worked with all kinds of animals at the zoo. From marsupials to elephants. One giraffe had a bad tooth that they had to take care of. She tended many of the babies. Her heart melted taking care of these innocent creatures.

April was busy. Her classes were usually from 8 a.m. to noon. Then she went home and had lunch with her neighbor. After lunch she went to work. She often showed up early to help out with the animals' lunchtime.

April's life was so full. She remembered to use a paperclip along the side of her calendar so she would remember to send postcards to her family. April was able to locate a church for her to attend and she liked many of the members. Many of the students she went to college also attended there.

After work April would study, sometimes until late into the night or wee hours of morning. Now she appreciated her frogman training more than ever. Often she only got four hours of sleep, but she felt invigorated, alive, and ready to tackle each day. From her apartment she walked to school and back home for lunch daily. To go to work she biked, she fastened a carrier she found in a junk pile onto her bike. She put one in the front and one on the back for stops at the store or for bringing home books or case study material.

April had made several friends very quickly. One she enjoyed more than others was Sue. Sue was studying to be a nurse. But she wanted more than anything to be a Vet, like April. April felt bad for her, but Sue was here on a scholarship and could not change her major. She encouraged Sue to keep going. She felt certain Sue would make an awesome nurse one day.

The two of them spent days biking together, discovering the city they were living in. Sue was always chatting. She had one brother who was older than she was, and it was obvious she loved him. Sue was always talking about him. Her parents were older, much older than April's. They were in their early seventies now and did not drive much anymore. Sue depended on her brother for news, but he did not like to write. So, every weekend either Sue called him, or he called her.

Many times April would help Sue to study. She was more of a hands-on person, but she had to know answers by words too, especially to pass her boards. It was painstaking studying, often

Sue would groan and hit the table. April thought it was funny, but Sue was easily frustrated. April loved to study. There were so many different animals, different body structures, chemistry, and blood types. So these two were often seen together either at the library, in the college hall, biking, or at April's apartment. Often Sue slept there if it was too dark for her to return to her dorm. She did not like studying at the dorm. It was too noisy, and she could not concentrate. Sue liked how quiet April's apartment was. No one bothered them there.

One day while biking, Sue's tire was beginning to go low. Thankfully there was a garage nearby. They pumped up the tire, but it did not hold.

One of the garage workers came to the girls and said they needed a patch for that tire. He was willing to take the tire off and fix it for her if she could pay the 15-dollar charge. April thought that was a little high, but they agreed. But they would have to come back tomorrow because they did not have 15 dollars between them.

"Okay," he said. "Your bike will be here. See you tomorrow or I will sell it."

"You wouldn't!" Sue said.

"If you don't come back, I will," he said.

"I will be here tomorrow," Sue reassured him.

"Now how are we going to get to the apartment with two people and one bike?" April asked.

"Like this," Sue said hopping onto the front handle bars.

"Whoa. I can't steer with you on there."

Sue got down and slid on the back rim. "How is this?" she asked laughing. "It's not that far. Let's at least try it," she said.

So they did. When they rounded the corner to head to April's apartment, they heard a siren. It was a police car. April pulled into the small yard at her apartment and the girls stood on the sidewalk.

"Can we help you officers?" Sue asked politely.

"You girls were riding that bicycle inappropriately. That is against the law. Did you know that?" the one officer responded.

"You're kidding?" Sue asked. She was really shocked.

"No. I am not kidding. I could haul your ass in on that offense. Don't give me a smart lip," he said.

April had a really bad feeling about this. "Please, officers, we are late for class. We do appreciate you being so attentive on your job, but excuse us please," and April pulled Sue down around corner and up the right side towards the college.

The officers followed them in their car, but they had to stop at the corner due to oncoming traffic.

The girls darted into thick shrubbery in front of a nearby house. They hid there as the police car turned and drove up the street very slowly looking for them. Once the officers passed and were up near the top of the street, the girls carefully left the bushes and ran to April's apartment. They hid the bike in her neighbor's shed.

When inside the apartment with the door locked and bolted, they breathed. "That was creepy," Sue said.

"It sure was. I did not like that at all. Making a big deal out of sitting on a bike should be the least of their problems. My Dad never would have done that," April said.

Before long Sue was asleep. She could sleep standing up, April thought. April could not sleep. This incident unnerved her. It did not seem right, and it bothered her deeply. Sue slept on the couch, so April headed upstairs to her bedroom, and returned with a blanket for Sue to cover with.

Upstairs in her bedroom with all the lights out, April heard noises outside her window. She pulled her curtain aside and there was that same police car with its lights flashing. One officer was out looking in the bushes with a flashlight, probably for the bike April thought. She was glad they put the bike in the shed and not on the back porch. Sure enough, a flashlight beam went around the side of the house to the back of the porch. April could hear a knock on the back door and her neighbor turned down her television to answer the door. April went downstairs to her kitchen so she could hear the conversation better through the dumbwaiter on the wall.

"Sorry to disturb you, Ma'am. Do you live here alone?"

"No. I do not. My son is sleeping upstairs, and my husband is out picking up milk at the store. How may I help you?" she asked.

"We are looking for two blonde girls who were on a bicycle near this house," he said.

"There are no blonde girls here. My son has no daughters. His son works swing shift and lives here too on the other side. And she motioned toward April's apartment.

"Does your grandson have a blonde girlfriend by chance?" the officer asked.

The neighbor said, "No. He does not. All he does is work, eat, and sleep. He has no time for a girlfriend. You must have the wrong house," she said.

"Okay then. So sorry to have bothered you, Ma'am. You have a lovely evening," the officer said.

"You too, Sir. Good night," her neighbor said.

April waited for the man to go back into his car. There was a connecting wall with a dumbwaiter that was intact. The neighbor could open it up and holler for April if she needed help. Now it was April who lifted the wooden frame. "Are you all right?" she asked.

"I am coming. I am coming," the older woman said. "I do not know what is going on, but he was no officer. He reeked of alcohol, his shirt was dirty, and the badge looked plastic. You be careful. If you can hide out and not be seen for a day or so, I doubt he will be back."

April thanked her and went to bed. It was a fitful sleep.

In the morning April told Sue what had happened. Sue wondered, "How am I going to get my bike?"

"Like this," April said. Again she went to the older woman's shared service window. "Are you there?" April asked. The woman appeared suddenly as she was in the kitchen having a warm tea. "I was wondering if you would do us a small favor. Sue had a flat tire. If she does not go and pay for the repair today, they are going to sell her bicycle. We can't go double. That is what brought the officers, or whatever they were, in the first place. Can you drive us to the garage?" April asked her.

"No. I can't drive so well anymore, but the car is good and registered with good tags. Why don't you drive my car and pick the bike up?"

"You would let me do that?" April questioned.

"Why wouldn't I? I like you, Kiddo, and your cooking," and they laughed. So after a quick breakfast April lent Sue fifteen dollars, and they walked to the neighbor's garage and drove the neighbor's Buick to the garage.

April looked around as they parked the Buick. There were no police cars in sight. Sue went in, paid for the repairs, and the garage man came out wheeling the bike to put it into the trunk for them.

"Thanks so much," April said.

"We are here to please," he replied.

"My neighbor was good to me and let me use this car. Do you mind if we make a quick stop at the store and pick up some things so I can cook her dinner?

"Let's go," Sue said. They made a quick stop in the back alley to put Sue's bike in the shed by April's, and then they went six blocks to the grocery store.

At the checkout, Sue looked out the big window at the front of the store, and she nudged April. April looked up and Sue's face was pale. She looked in the direction Sue was looking and outside in front of the store was that same police car.

April paid for the groceries, but the girls did not want to go outside. They sat on the bench in front of the store. Sue felt so scared she almost vomited. "We are all right. They did not see us, and they don't know we are using a car. Take a deep breath." April got up to look and damn they were still sitting there. April had classes in a half hour and had to go. "Listen you stay here. I will have someone get your bike to you. I have to go. I will go."

Sue grabbed April's arm, "Don't go. Stay here, the hell with the class."

Just then a group of guys came through and April stopped them with tears in her eyes. "Hey, Guys. Can you please help us? We are being harassed by those cops out there. We have not done anything wrong. They are stalking us. I have to be at my class in a half hour, and we are afraid to go out. That is Sue, her bike is in the truck of our neighbor's car that she let us use, and . . ."

"Hold on a second. You", he pointed to Sue. "You go with these two. Jake take off your coat and give it to her." The coat was a long trench coat with a big hood. "You put that on and hide your hair and face and go with them. You go with me, Bob, Seth, and Geoff. They will never notice you." He put his arm around April, and he towered over her. He put his scarf around her neck and head, easily hiding her hair. The three others came with them like a school of fish. Once near his car, April and her escort got in. The other two walked past the police car as a distraction and called the men in the car, PIGS.

One of the officers became agitated and pulled out his stick to chase and hit the boys. They laughed at them as April's escort stopped at the Buick and let her out. "Keep the scarf. Give it back to me when you see me again," he said to her and winked.

"Thanks. I owe you," April replied.

"Get going," he said as he looked in his rear-view mirror.

April backed up and her escort did not allow any other cars to get near her. She left the lot and parked in her neighbor's garage, safe and unseen. Later she sent a text to Sue and asked if she was all right.

"Dang straight. I got my bike and a date," she sent a message back.

April tried to relaxed and pay attention in class, but she was unnerved. When she was out of class, she reported what had happened to the school office. They radioed the town police to alert them and to verify whether it was or was not them. It was not them, but now the police were aware of the situation.

April felt better. She walked with some other students all the way to her apartment. Once there, she had lunch with her neighbor and told her what had happened at the grocery store.

"You be careful. There are nuts out there," the elderly woman said.

"I will. I just can't understand what I did," April said.

The elderly woman touched April's hand. "You did nothing. For whatever the reason, idiots make targets, Maybe they had you in their bullseye or maybe it was your friend Sue. Maybe they have now moved on to someone else. It's obvious they were looking, that is most likely what they were doing at the store."

April felt sick. It was a very dark, disturbing feeling. She had to go to work and to get there, she had to ride her bike. She voiced her concerns to her neighbor.

"Not today," she said. "I'm driving you. So watch out world, Edie is coming out," and she laughed.

Edie was not a bad driver. She was distracted a lot. April got to school and home. Not once did she see the "cops." She went to bed with a clear head and went to sleep fast. Tomorrow was the end of the school week, and she was looking forward this weekend to work at the zoo.

Before they left April told her neighbor she wanted to call her Father to call her Father to let him know what had happened. "Absolutely, call him. He should know," Edie said. April dialed her Dad at the office. "Dad, it's me April. I am having a little problem and wanted you to know," she said.

After she told her Dad what had happened, her Father had a tight feeling in his chest. "April did you notify the school and the police?" he asked her.

"Yes, Dad. I did. I don't want to miss class or work because if I don't go, I will fall behind."

Her Dad said, "Just stay in your apartment for a while, what would be the difference if you were sick?" April agreed, but she told him the zoo really needed help and helping them helped her so much, she would forget about her problem.

"Don't go, not for a few days April. Let this settle down and they might give up or move on," her Dad told her.

"Okay, Dad. I will think about it and go from there," she said.

"If you need me don't hesitate to call me. Use your cell phone," he said.

"I will Dad. I will," and then she hung up.

"Are you ready to boogie?" Edie said chuckling. April admired her neighbor so much, her willingness to help, She had not driven for a while, but just like riding a bike, it comes back quickly. The reason she had stopped driving was all the increased traffic.

They both hopped into Edie's car, her neighbor pressed the remote button to the garage door, and it opened. She backed the Buick out to the alley. Then she pressed the button to the garage door again to close. She turned the car into the alley way, and they were off. "Good heavens! I have not been out this way for a long time. Just look how things have changed," Edie said out loud.

The drive was short, just a few blocks. April got out and thanked Edie as she closed her door. "Do you want me to pick you up?" Edie asked her.

"No, I should be fine. It may be late and maybe someone here will drop me off," April told her.

On the ride home with her supervisor, he told April he would pick her up the next morning, since it was Friday, and she always came in on Friday mornings. Just wait inside the door, he would see her tomorrow at 7 a.m. Just wait inside and I will toot my horn," he told her. April was glad it sure took a lot of stress off of her.

April and her neighbor had a nice chat. Then April left for her own apartment and had a nice relaxing shower. That evening she read a lot of required reading material and studied some charts of animal structures, with her tomato soup. When she looked at her watch it was almost 11 p.m.

April was tired. She went upstairs and took another hot shower and then got her clothing laid out and then she peeked out of her window. It was snowing like crazy. It was near the end of November, and not unusual weather, but it would make a mess in the morning. April pulled out a heavy sweater and her boots to take along with her. She slept soundly and was up at 5 a.m.

April had her backpack ready, she was dressed and waiting at her door at 6:45 a.m. As time dragged on, April was concerned her supervisor would not see her. There were now other cars parked at the curb, so there was no room to pull another car in front of her apartment.

April looked at her watch, it was 7:10. She gathered up her things and waited a few more minutes. Then she stepped outside to stand on her step so she could look left, down the street to where her supervisor would be coming from.

April never saw the blue cruiser two cars up from her apartment. It was sitting there idling, waiting for her. As April was looking left for her supervisor, a man got out of the blue cruiser on her right side and grabbed her, throwing her off balance to the cement. He kicked her and pummeled her to put her into the back of their car. April was shocked. She kicked and hit him with her fists. She gouged his eyes and hit his nose upwards to break it.

The man flinched but did not stop. He pulled her one arm forcefully up behind her back twisting it. "Get in the car," he said. He shoved April into the back seat of the patrol car and slammed the door. He got in on the driver's side, watched for oncoming traffic, and pulled the car out onto the road.

In the oncoming traffic was April's supervisor. He did see a blue cruiser pull away from the curb three cars in front of him. He saw April's backpack by the curb along with one of her gloves. Since he did not see what happened, he thought April dropped one of her gloves, but was waiting inside. He parked his car, put the flashers on, got out, and knocked at April's apartment door. There was no answer.

He then studied the outside near the backpack, there were shoe marks in the snow all over, as if there had been a scuffle. A human body print was on the side walk, laying down. He noticed blood on the curb, he pulled out his cell phone and called the police.